Underneath
It All

What My Life Was Like as an
Enlisted Man on a Nuclear Submarine

Coming soon by Bill Carbary

Think Like Gods

Underneath
It All

What My Life Was Like as an Enlisted Man on a Nuclear Submarine

Bill Carbary EM1 (SS) / William G. Carbary / "Bill"

and

Liam

Published by Bill Carbary

Cover design by: Roger Seward

Printed by CreateSpace

Printed in the United States of America

ISBN-13: 978-0692061510

ISBN-10: 0692061517

Dedicated to
The Crew of the USS Sculpin (SSN-590)

Prologue

Except for some editing, the words in the story to come were written in the early 1970s. I was known as *Bill* or *Carbary* during that time.

I was an enlisted naval sailor stationed aboard the USS Sculpin (SSN 590) during the 1960s. I was in my early twenties when I experienced the backdrop of this story and my late twenties when I wrote this story.

I intended this story to fall under the category of *fiction*. There is some truth in this, as I made some shit up. The easy part of writing this story, however, was how much of it I didn't make up.

The story is told in chapter by chapter drama, dialogue with linear continuity, *and* in chapter by chapter verse with philosophical continuity.

The protagonist (Bill) and antithesis-protagonist (Parsons) reflect off each other as does one's image and mirror image (left is right, and right is left).

Bill knows but pretends he doesn't; Parsons doesn't know but pretends he does.

This estrangement of self is described in verse in Chapter VI:

> *Most of me accepts the joke*
> *And laughter is the pay*
> *Most of me believes that it*
> *Is really the best way*
> *And it's most of me*
> *That will keep on going*
> *And not listen very long*
> *To the part of me that*
> *Believes there's more*
> *And wonders what went wrong*

Co-author, Liam, contributes the title, the story undercurrent, and some verses. The Liam psyche has been with Bill since conscious awareness and continues even to the writing of this prologue.

UNDERNEATH IT ALL

> *Build us a world of shelter*
> *Make it straight and tall*
> *Cushion the floor and make it soft*
> *To protect us when we fall*
> *And take some pictures of our fantasies*
> *And pin them to the wall*
> *And we'll live in that world and never look*
> *Underneath it all*
>
> —*Liam*

Chapter I

If you join the navy
And you probably will
And you don't want to be
Just a run of the mill
Tell your recruiter you want to be…
A pre-vert…pre-vert…pre-vert…pre-vert
Sub-ma-rine…
Pre-vert…pre-vert…pre-vert

—Radio Station: S.T.U.D.

I

5/27/1966

It had taken about twenty minutes to reach the base from the airport. Bill sat in the backseat staring out the window for most of the way. He knew that he should have been noticing the street signs and houses. It wasn't that his mind was occupied with other things, he just couldn't seem to concentrate. Bill did look at a few palm trees. He had never seen palm trees before, so he looked at them. It was about the only deliberate thing he did on the way.

"Here it is," the cab driver said as he turned into the parking area.

Bill squared his white hat on top of his head and looked around. Only a few scattered cars occupied the huge parking lot, and at the far end, barracks-styled buildings, squatting on concrete blocks, appeared empty and unwanted.

The cab pulled up in front of a row of vending machines. Tucked inside a three-sided wooden enclosure, the machines faced away from the noisy, rolling waves only a few yards away and about six feet down. Next to the enclosure, three tall, skinny, aluminum telephone booths stood side by side; they too were facing away from the noisy sea. In the center booth, a sailor sat on the small wooden seat. He wore blue navy dungarees and a blue grease-stained working jacket with tattered sleeves and a torn pocket. His face was shadowed by the brim of a baseball cap.

Bill watched him as he fed money into the vertical slot mouth of the shiny telephone. He could still hear the clanking of the coins, as he looked beyond the booths at the giant ship, anchored several hundred yards off shore, silhouetted against the blue white-capped expanse of the harbor.

The ship appeared immense. The gray welded steel plates of her hull rose up out of the water like a wall and reached up to what seemed like a hundred feet before their continuity was broken by a steel railing stretching across the first deck. On the bow of the ship, the number AS-17 was painted in large, white, block-styled figures. Bill searched for the elongated gray barrels of the huge guns, which (from his experience with plastic models) he considered to be common to all navy ships. All he saw were several cranes reaching out over the side of the top deck and numerous rows of black rubber cables stretching out over the railing and connecting the large gray giant with the smaller ships below.

Bill knew the smaller ships to be submarines, and he was awed that they looked so small when compared to the larger ship, which he later learned was called a sub-tender. There were three submarines nestled abreast of each other on the dock side of the tender. Unlike the tender, which stood rigid and unmoving as if embedded in the mud, the submarines slowly rolled and bobbed with the moving sea, and they seemed to be like dependent babies clinging to the protection of a huge metal mother.

The two inboard submarines were the conventional kind, the type Bill had seen in many world war two submarine movies. They looked like miniature ships, with a small flat deck only a few feet above the water line from the pointed bow to the blunted stern. In the center of the subs, flat, rectangular-shaped structures rose up like black rigid sails and housed the numerous antennas, masts, and periscopes that peeked out over the top.

The outboard sub, Bill knew to be the newer kind. This was a "nuke." It didn't have a flat deck, nor did it appear to have a distinguishable bow or stern. It stuck up out of the water like the back of a turtle. Sticking up from the center was a structure like the "conning towers" on the old subs only it had what looked like short "wings" extending from both sides. Bill wondered if that was "his" submarine, and at the same time, he hoped that it wasn't. He found himself wishing that "his" submarine was out at sea, and that he wouldn't have to go aboard right away.

His leave had gone so fast. It seemed like just yesterday when he left nuclear power training in Idaho. Up until now, it had always been "in the future" when he would have to go aboard a submarine. But, suddenly, the future was now, and he was here and everything looked so foreign and lonely and....

"... Ballast Point?" The cab driver was looking at him expectantly as he pushed down the lever on his money meter.

"Huh?" Bill said.

"You did want to go to Ballast Point, didn't you?"

"Uh... sure." Bill looked toward the subs. "Do you know which... uh... how do I..."

The driver opened the door and walked to the rear of the cab. Bill scooped up the large manila envelope that lay on the seat beside him and opened his door. He stepped out and watched the driver, as he removed the large sea-bag from the truck.

"That will be $4.60," the driver said, as he placed the bag on the ground.

Bill searched through his wallet and pulled out five one-dollar bills. "Here, keep it."

"Thanks." The driver motioned with his head over to his left. "Ask him. He'll tell ya."

The driver turned and slid back into the cab, and Bill stood facing a small guard shack sitting on the parking lot end of the pier. Against the shack, a sailor casually propped his body and stood facing in Bill's direction.

Only one of his feet was flat on the ground: his left leg, bent at the knee, crossed over in front of his right supporting leg, and the toe of his left shoe rested against and pointed into the blacktop. Both hands were flat against his stomach, palms in, and buried knuckle deep by the buttoned waist of his trousers.

Bill stood motionless. He wondered if the sailor was looking at him or if he just happened to be facing in his direction. It would be easier, Bill thought, if there could have been someone here to order him forward or if he could just march ahead. Not that Bill particularly liked to march, but marching did produce a certain hypnotic effect that seemed to erase in his mind any thought of a destination or even memories of where he had started from. He refocused his eyes on the sailor, hesitated a moment longer, and then stooped down and grasped the sea-bag. He lifted the bag to his shoulder and started in the direction of the guard shack. *One-two, one-two, one-two,* he thought as his feet pounded down on the blacktop.

II

Bill placed his bag on the ground and stood before the sailor. "I'm reporting aboard the USS Sculpin."

"We all got our problems," the sailor said. A slight grin appeared on his face.

Bill looked at the ground and then back up at the sailor. He glanced at his left arm and noticed the one V-shaped chevron below his rate designation. *A third-class ship fitter,* he thought. Bill was conscious of the rating patch on his own arm. He, too, was only a third class. The man couldn't possibly know that he was almost second. *He probably even thinks he's senior,* Bill thought. He noticed the night stick at the sailor's side, which was holstered by a loop in the wide, white military guard belt he wore around his waist. *It wouldn't matter anyway,* Bill thought. *He has the authority of a watch stander; the bastard knows it, too.*

Bill removed a piece of paper from the pouch in the manila envelope. "Uh... I was supposed to report aboard at four... uh... sixteen hundred. My name's Carbary. Maybe you have my name on a list or something?"

The sailor just stared at him, and he ignored the piece of paper that Bill held out in front of his face. His grin grew more noticeable.

Bill's face flushed. "Look, just tell me where to go."

The sailor motioned with his thumb over his shoulder toward the sub-tender. "The Sculpin's out there."

"I could have figured that out for myself. Do they come and get me or what?" Bill paused and lowered his voice. "I know I'm a little early. Do I have to wait till sixteen hundred or can you call them, or what?"

The sailor took a deep breath and let it out slowly. He shook his head as if he were suddenly bored with the conversation. He turned and walked into the shack and sat down on a small wooden stool. As he reached for a magazine on the counter, he looked up at Bill. "There's a liberty launch every half-hour, should be another in 'bout …oh… (he looked at his watch) …ten minutes." He motioned to his right. "They leave from the float down there."

Bill looked down at the float and then back at the sailor. "Thanks for nothing," he said as he reached down for his bag.

Bill dragged the sea-bag down to the float and sat down on it, facing out toward the tender. The float slowly moved up and down, and Bill felt his stomach becoming a little uneasy. He felt both ashamed and scared that he seemed to be becoming seasick just from the slight movements caused by a few small waves. He fought back the urge to stick his head over the edge and barf in the water. He reasoned that the excitement and strain of traveling, and the worry of what lay ahead, was probably the primary cause for his weak stomach. But underneath this reasoning, there was a fear that maybe he had made a mistake by joining the navy.

It had been over two years since Bill had enlisted. It was not something that he had planned—it had been just one of those things that happened almost by accident. He had intended to join the marines. At least he had intended to talk about joining the marines. His father wanted him to talk to the marine recruiter, and that was what he had gone down to the post office to do. He now understood that he should have called first, but he had never considered the possibility that the recruiter wouldn't be there.

He wondered how many other would-be marines (or army or air force men for that matter) got trapped the same way. He had never considered it before, but it amused him to consider that the navy recruiter had some sort of spy network that informed him when potential victims were near his lair. How did he just 'happen' to be walking by when Bill was knocking on the marine recruiter's door? And what a line! He could tell right away that Bill was too smart to be a marine.

Hell, he hadn't even been smart enough to know that the navy recruiter was a "chief" rather than a sergeant. And, after the results of the tests came back, it was obvious (at least to the recruiter) that Bill was even too smart for the ordinary navy. Bill was amazed to learn that the test results proved him to be among the elite or the "one in a thousand" who had the potential to become a technician in the Nuclear Submarine Navy. Of course, his father was disappointed that he hadn't joined the marines, but he had somewhere heard that one had to be tough to be in submarines; therefore, he grudgingly accepted the navy as better than nothing.

Here he was. He had enlisted for six years so he would qualify for all the special schools the navy would send him to. That had been the hooker. Many times, Bill wondered if the only thing special about him was that he had been especially gullible. He did, however, go to a number of schools. First, he went to electrician's school, then submarine school, then basic nuclear-power school, and, finally, nuclear power prototype training in Idaho. And he did well. He was always at or near the top of his class in all the schools he attended. There was, however, always a suspicion in the back of his mind that he was getting the short end of the stick. He also got plenty of feedback that he wasn't alone in feeling this way. In all the places he had been, he always found men who would bitch and complain and liken the navy to a big vacuum machine that was trying to suck them in and pull them under. Bill, though, was never a bitcher. He just worried. Now, as he sat waiting for the boat to come and take him out to the nuclear navy, he felt a concentrated knot of tension lodged in his stomach, and he wondered if it would all prove to be worth it, and he worried that he might have made a mistake.

III

"Which one you reporting aboard to?"

Bill looked around. The sailor he had seen in the phone booth was standing behind him. He stood with his feet apart and both thumbs hooked into the front pockets of his dungarees. Bill noticed the blue stringy threads hanging from the sleeves of his jacket, and he could smell the grease and oil that stained his clothes. Bill looked at his left arm and found no rating patch. Must *be a seaman,* he thought.

"Sculpin," Bill said. "You on one of the boats?" Bill had talked to submariners before, and he knew that they called them "boats."

The sailor squatted down and looked out at the submarines. He pushed his baseball cap to the back of his head, turned toward Bill, and smiled. "Yup."

"Which one?"

He was still smiling, and Bill recognized that it was something different from a friendly smile. It seemed more like an "I know something that you don't know" type of smile.

"Sculpin."

Bill wasn't sure whether to believe him or not. He looked the sailor over again. "I thought the nukes were pretty clean?" Bill wouldn't have said that if the sailor had been a petty officer. But he was only a seaman, and Bill was almost a second, and…

The sailor laughed out loud. He slapped both his knees with the palms of his hands and stood up. "Oh, they are. They are." He reached out and started thumping with his forefinger on the top of Bill's white hat. "And you're going to be one of the rags that helps keep them that way."

Bill stood up and removed his white hat. He examined the grease smudges the sailor had thumped into the crown. He beat the hat against his thigh and stood looking at the other man. "Now, why'd ya do that?"

"Name's Parsons," the sailor said. His smile had digressed to the same type of grin the pier guard had displayed.

Bill squared his hat back on top of his head. He still wondered if Parsons was really aboard the Sculpin. "Mine's Carbary."

Parsons's broad smile reappeared, and it even looked friendly. He held out his hand. "What's your first name?"

Bill eyed his greasy hand, hesitated a moment, and then reached for it. "Bill, what's yours?"

Parsons snapped his hand away. "Fuck you, Bill," he said as he burst into laughter.

Bill's face flushed red. For just a half a moment, he stared at Parsons with narrowed eyes and tightened jaw. He started to say something but stopped. Finally, he released his breath, shook his head, and joined Parsons' laughter. Parsons slapped him several times on the back, and Bill knew that the white striping, which was on his collar flap, was becoming greasy.

"You're all right," Parsons said.

"Yeah." Bill watched the approach of the liberty launch. He turned to Parsons. "You sure you're on the Sculpin?"

IV

The liberty launch did not go directly out to the submarines as Bill had expected. Instead, it went all the way around to the far side of the tender. There were a couple of other sailors who came down to ride the launch out, and Bill noticed that they seemed to move to the far end of the boat away from him and Parsons. Bill didn't know who had moved away from whom, as he had merely followed Parsons onto the launch. He sensed, though, that it was a kind of mutual avoidance, and he later learned that the best that could ever be expected was a rather uneasy truce between the "bubbleheads" and the "surface skimmers."

Parsons didn't say anything during the trip to the tender. Bill wanted to start up a conversation, but he didn't know what to say. He had almost asked him where his hometown was and how long had he been in the navy, but he somehow sensed that Parsons would consider these as stupid questions and laugh at him. Several times, he caught Parsons looking at him, but as soon as he looked back, Parsons would quickly turn away.

The launch arrived alongside of a float moored abreast of the tender, and Bill stared up at what the navy called a "ladder" of about two hundred steps leading to the first deck. The ladder was an open steel staircase that ascended the immense grey wall by reversing the direction of incline twice. At the top of the ladder, the quarterdeck area was just about directly above the float. Bill looked at Parsons. "You mean I have to carry this goddamned sea-bag all the way up there?"

"You don't think I'm going to do it, do you? Of course, you could go up and ask the deck watch to have a crane hoist it up for you."

"Do you think they...you son-of-a-bitch! You'd get a kick out of that, wouldn't ya?"

"Just trying to help out." Parsons removed his wallet from his pocket and took out his I.D. card. "Here, give me your service record. I'll carry that." Bill handed him the manila envelope, and Parsons jumped from the boat seat onto the float and started up the ladder.

Bill hoisted the sea-bag onto his shoulder and stepped up on the seat of the boat. He put one foot on the rail of the boat and pushed hard to lift himself and the bag over the railing onto the float. As he stepped out to the float, the boat moved away, and he quickly lunged forward to keep from falling into the water. His sea-bag tipped forward, and he stumbled across the float like a football player tackling a sand bag. If the sea-bag hadn't been in front of his feet, he would have stepped into the gap between the float and the tender. As it was, the bag merely thudded against the tender hull and cushioned the impact on his shoulder.

As he straightened up, he could hear Parsons laughing from above on the ladder. "Walk much?"

Bill readjusted the sea-bag on his shoulder and looked at Parsons. "Get laid!" he said.

"You talk like a man with no white hat," Parsons said, as he continued up the ladder.

"Huh?" Bill reached to his head, but as he was doing it, he realized the effort was unnecessary. Floating a couple of feet from the edge of the float, his hat bobbed in the water. It was close enough for him to still see the smudges on the top of the crown, but too far away to reach. He looked around for something long enough to snare it with. Nothing. He cursed, shook his head, and started up the ladder.

When he finally reached the top, he flopped the bag onto the deck and leaned against the railing. He wiped the sweat from his forehead with the back of his hand and stood drawing deep breaths, not yet aware of the first class who was staring at him from across the quarterdeck.

Bill heard a voice bellow out, "Where'd *you* come from?"

"Huh?"

"You're not in the navy, I hope?"

"I...I...."

"Where? Never mind. You got an I.D. card?"

Bill reached in his back pocket and pulled out his wallet. He quickly fingered through the various cards and papers. He went through once and started over. The first class watched him impatiently. "Here it is!" Bill displayed a grin as he held out the card.

"What t'hellya grinning for? Ya want a medal for finding your I.D. card? Where's your liberty card?"

"My liberty...oh...well, I don't have one...uh...I mean I'm reporting aboard...."

"You mean you're reporting in, in this condition?"

"...the Sculpin."

"That explains it," he said as he eyed Bill again. "Where's your hat, sailor?"

"Uh...down there," Bill said thumbing back and down toward the water.

The first class took a deep breath and released it, and Bill noticed that he now looked like a man who was performing a disagreeable task. He slouched to the side and rested his elbow against a podium that held an open log book. "Okay, let's see your orders."

Bill quickly looked around, "Uh...."

The first class straightened up and leaned slightly forward. "You do have your orders, don't you? Or are they 'down there' too?"

"No," Bill was still looking around. "Parsons carried them up for me."

The first class was smiling. "Aw, were they too heavy? WHO THE HELL'S PARSONS?" he bellowed.

Bill wondered if he had been a would-be marine too. "He's the guy who came up before me. You must have seen him. He was wearing dungarees and carrying my service record and—"

The first class was shaking his head. "Uh, you're beautiful. Let's see your I.D. card again."

Bill again pulled out his wallet and located the card. The first class took it and called a seaman over who had a white belt on like the sailor on the pier.

"Call up topside to the Sculpin and find out if they're expecting a third class electrician, name of...(he looked at the I.D. card) Carbary."

The seaman walked away, and the first class stood watching Bill. He had a grin on his face, and he held his hands behind his back as he rocked back and forth from his heels to his toes. "Let me tell you something, buddy. You picked the wrong ship. You're not going to get away with anything here." He continued rocking, still grinning and watching Bill intently. "Especially when I have the watch."

Just then Parsons walked around the corner of an adjacent passageway. "Goddamn it...(he looked at the envelope he held in his hand) Carbary...you think I've get all day to wait for you while you're up here shooting the shit." He didn't quite manage to suppress the grin that pulled at the corners of his mouth.

"You son-of-a-bitch," Bill said as he grabbed the envelope. He reached into the pocket and pulled out his orders. "Here they are," he said, thrusting his hand out. He almost hit the first class in the chest.

The first class grabbed the paper and quickly scanned it. Bill noticed that he hardly even looked at it. *That son-of-a-bitch knew all along,* he thought.

He handed the paper hack to Bill. "I'll remember you. You better not cross my quarterdeck again without a white hat."

Bill replaced the orders in the envelope pocket, and with his free hand in the handle of the sea-bag, he lifted the bag so that the bottom was resting on his knee.

Parsons held out his hand. "Here, I'll carry your records."

"Like hell you will. Here, you can carry...this!" He pushed the bag with his knee, toward Parsons.

Parsons caught the bag with both arms and lifted it up to his shoulder. "Whatever's right," he said as he turned and followed Bill down the passageway. "You know where you're going?"

Bill stopped, and Parsons passed him and started around the corner. "How come you let that skimmer get on you like that?" he said just loud enough for the first class to hear.

Bill Followed Parsons down a ladder that led to a machinery space. When Parsons reached the bottom, he flopped the bag down onto the deck.

"What's the matter, you tired?" Bill asked.

Parsons sat down on the sea-bag. "No, just waiting for you to catch up." He slapped the bag with his hand. "Whaddaya got in here anyway? You know you're not allowed to bring civilian clothes aboard, don't you?"

"I figured that. I left them at a locker club downtown."

"Downtown? Now, that's dumb. There's a locker club right here on base."

"Well, I didn't know that. What's it to you, anyway?"

"Doesn't matter. You can always change later. What'd ya have in here anyway?"

"Just my navy gear."

"Your navy gear? I knew it! Straight from boot camp. I bet you even have everything stenciled. Look, you're going aboard a submarine. Even if you get your own bunk and locker, which is not very likely, you won't have room for a quarter of this stuff. Parsons looked at the bag. "I bet you even brought your P-coat, and your raincoat, and a set of galoshes your mother told you to wear in case it rained."

"Why didn't you tell me this before I dragged this thing all the way out here?"

Parsons shrugged. "I wasn't carrying it then."

"And what do you mean I won't get a locker? Do you have a locker?"

"Of course I've got a locker." Parsons looked annoyed.

"Well, I'm senior to you. If you have a locker, why shouldn't I get a locker?"

"How do you know you're senior to me? Just because I don't wear a patch on my arm and go around sticking it under everybody's nose doesn't mean I'm not rated. Christ, I've spent more time backing down submerged than you've spent in the navy. Even if you were senior, it wouldn't matter." Parsons picked up a nut he found on the deck next to his foot and tossed it toward the box of scrap iron sitting next to the lathe.

"I can't figure you at all," Bill said.

"If you think I'm taking you by the hand, forget it. All's I'm doing is protecting myself. Hell, left on your own, you might leave your bag lying around in the third level, and I might come back from the beach drunk and trip over it." Parsons stared at Bill. "Something the matter with your eyes?"

Bill looked down and his face reddened. "No...uh...well, I can see all right. I just have a weak eye muscle. It's called strabismus."

"Oh yeah? Well as long as you can see, I guess that's all that's important, huh?" Parsons picked up the sea-bag and put it on his shoulder. "C'mon Crazy Eyes, let's go down to your new home."

As Parsons walked down the brow from the tender to the first sub, Bill noticed that he flashed his right hand in front of his forehead. He wasn't sure if Parsons was swatting a bug or saluting, but he figured he'd better be safe and do the same. Parsons must have caught the motion out of the corner of his eye as he stepped off the brow, for he turned and stared at him just as he brought his hand down. "Look, stupid, you don't salute with no hat on. If you feel patriotic, hold your hard over your heart or something." Parsons laughed.

The Sculpin was the outboard sub, so they had to cross the two older boats first. Each of the subs was guarded by a topside watch who was armed with a forty-five automatic. Bill half expected to be challenged by the watches, or at least made to explain why he had no white hat, but they merely nodded to Parsons and seemed to ignore him altogether.

When they arrived on the rounded hull of the Sculpin, Parsons flopped the sea-bag down and smiled at the topside watch. "Got a live one for you, Murray."

Murray glanced casually at Bill and picked up his log book. "Name?"

Before Bill could speak, Parsons answered. "Crazy Eyes Carbary."

Murray started writing and Bill walked over and looked. <u>13:30 Carbary, C.E.</u>

Murray looked at Bill's rating patch. <u>EM3.</u>

"Service number?"

"698 44 38"

<u>698 44 38</u>, <u>reported aboard</u>.

"Is the chief of the boat down below?" Parsons asked.

"Yeah, I think he's down in the chief's quarters. Or, he might be in the crew's mess; they're showing a flick."

"Oh yeah? Any good?"

"Naw, some Audie Murphy shitkicker. *Son of Destry* or something like that. I don't know why they can't get any good flicks. Audie Murphy's been on here so many times, he's ready for his walk through."

"Well, I'm going to take C.E. here down below to check in. Too bad you got the duty. A bunch of us are going over to the Pump Room later."

"Yeah, well that's the way it goes."

"What time we leaving tomorrow? You see the P.O.D. (plan of the day) yet?"

"Yeah, 'bout seven I think. Anyway, liberty expires at 0600."

Bill's heart jumped. "We're going to sea tomorrow?" he asked.

Parsons laughed and started down the forward hatch. "Isn't that what you came for? I'll get down below and you hand down your sea-bag."

Parsons disappeared down the hatch and Bill stood staring at the hole. "How long we going to be out?" he hollered down the hatch.

No answer.

He turned to Murray. "How lone we going to be out?"

If Murray heard him, he didn't indicate it.

Parsons shouted from down below. "You going to lower that goddamned bag of yours or not? I've got better things to do, you know!"

Chapter II

Oh, I'd rather be beaten till I'm lumpy and red
I'd rather be flailed and kicked in the head
I'd sooner be pounded all over the place
Even Snorkel Patty could sit on my face
Yes, I'd rather have torture, and I'd gladly take all
Than to have to start over and be a non-qual

—Radio Station: S.T.U.D.

I

When Bill reached the bottom of the ladder, Parsons was at the far end of the torpedo room standing by the watertight door leading into the crew's mess. "Might's well leave your bag where it is for now, at least until the cob gives you a hot bunk where you can store what gear you need."

"What's a hot bu—"

Parsons disappeared through the door.

Bill uneasily eyed two long, green cigar-shaped torpedoes that were supported on racks on both sides of the narrow passageway leading toward the crew's mess. He turned around and looked at his sea-bag, which sat on the deck behind the ladder and between two torpedo tube loading doors that extended out from the forward bulkhead. He could see his face in the polished brass doors. He shrugged and started toward the crew's mess.

The passageway in the crew's mess was not located in the center of the room as in the torpedo room, but, rather, was situated next to the port bulkhead. On the starboard side of the passageway, four parallel tables reached across to the opposite bulkhead. Padded benches, long enough for four men, stretched along the side of each table.

At the forward end of the room, a movie screen had been pulled down from the overhead, and the men sat facing this screen on the four rows of after benches. The forward benches had been shoved under the tables, and the men were able to lean back by pushing the after benches back and utilizing the forward bench pads as back cushions.

The lights were on and the men were sitting up when Bill entered. At the far end of the mess, next to the after-galley bulkhead, a chief sat on the last bench putting a new reel of film on the movie projector. Parsons was standing in the passageway talking to one of the men.

"...he was here when the movie started," the seated man said, "but I don't think he could handle it. He must be down in the chief's quarters." He looked at Bill. "Hmmmmm...we get a new mess cook, I see. Looks like a nuke. They make the worst kind too. Got no respect. Hey, you a nuke?"

Someone else spoke up. "He's got to be a nuke. That's the only kind of electrician they send aboard here."

"Goddamned nukes!"

"You noseconers are all alike," Parsons said. "All you ever do is sit around on your ass all day and bitch about the nukes." He started walking away. "C'mon C.E., let's go down to the chief's quarters."

"Hey Parsons, how come you didn't call your girlfriend from the boat? 'fraid someone might hear ya sweet-talking her?"

"He's just selfish. Wants to keep her all to himself. Some shipmate he is!"

"Hey, New Guy....What's his name, Parsons?"

"Crazy Eyes. C.E. for short."

"Hey C.E., ya know what a *good shipmate* is?"

"No."

"A sailor who goes onto the beach, gets two blow jobs, and brings one back and gives it to his buddy who has the duty."

[Laughter.]

"Look, he's blushing. Awwwww, ain't that cute? I bet he's cherry."

"Me first!"

"You stick with Parsons, C.E., he'll show ya how."

"How's he going to show him anything? He couldn t even make out with his own girlfriend. What's a matter, Parsons, she too busy to see ya?"

Parsons turned and smiled. "I wasn't calling my girlfriend; I was calling your wife. And you're right, she was too busy—but she put my name on the list."

"Yeah, right below two marines and a police dog," another voice added.

II

Bill caught up with Parsons, as he started down the ladder to the third level. "Hey, wait, I didn't know you were a nuke too."

"You never asked."

"Was that guy only kidding? I mean about me being a mess cook."

Parsons only smiled.

"And how did they know about you making a phone call? Did you tell them before you left?"

"What are ya doin'? writing a book? If you must know, someone must have been spying through the periscope. You were no surprise to them either."

* * *

Parsons continued down the ladder and stopped at the bottom next to a wooden door. He knocked twice and entered. Bill followed him into a small room. When he closed the door behind him, he immediately felt packaged by the compact compartment. The bulkheads on both sides of him were close enough so that he could reach out and press his palms flat against them, and he had to fight off the momentary urge to do so.

He was aware of the overhead, only a few inches above his hair, and glancing downward toward the polished linoleum deck didn't help; it only seemed to deepen the tingling sensation penetrating the top of his scalp—he knew he didn't need to slouch over, but he did anyway. Embedded in the bulkheads were ventilation pipes, lockers, and drawers and two dulled aluminum washbasins were folded face-in to a precisely designed space and the bowls bulged out and appeared as two huge opaque eyeballs. For an instant, Bill felt the panic of being trapped inside the head of a living creature, and he searched the clouded eyes desperately for a clue to its personality, but he found none.

"Got a hot one for you, Cob (chief of the boat)," Parsons said.

Bill had assumed that there would be someone else in the room when he had entered, but the room itself had temporarily absorbed his attention. He squeezed around to the side of Parsons and stood looking at a heavy-set, bald chief who was sitting at a table tucked into the far forward corner of the room.

The chief had a pen in his hand, and spread before him on the table was a scattered array of papers. He continued writing as the two men stood before him. Finally, he looked up at Bill. "Name?"

"Car—"

"Crazy Eyes Carbary," Parsons interrupted.

The chief removed a clipboard that was hanging from a hook on the bulkhead. He started writing on it, and Bill knew that he was writing "Carbary, C.E., but he also sensed that if he protested it would likely do more harm than good.

Parsons nudged him on the shoulder, "You're on your own, C.E. We'll be going back onto the beach in about…oh… (he looked at his watch)…make it eight o'clock. We'll be in the crew's mess about ten minutes to. If you want to go, you'd better not be late, because the liberty launch leaves on the hour." Parsons turned and opened the door. "Take it easy on him, Cob, he's tender." He looked again at Bill, puckered up his lips, made an exaggerated kissing sound, and then disappeared out the door.

"Let's see your orders," the cob said.

Bill removed the paper from the pouch and handed it to him. The cob looked it over and then looked up.

"Third-class nuke, huh? Well, you won't be working back aft for a while. You'll be taking Johnson's place mess-cooking." He paused a moment and then added, "Johnson's a third-class nuke too, he'll be going back aft now."

Bill was tempted to announce that he was almost second, but he thought better of it. "Where will I sleep?" he asked. He dreaded the answer he now felt sure was coming.

The cob looked at him impatiently. "I'm getting to that," he said. He lifted the first page on the clipboard and examined the page underneath. He made a few quick marks on the paper and then looked back up at Bill. "You'll be hot-bunking with Stewart. He's married, so he won't be using his rack when we're in port except when he has duty. At sea, he has the twelve-to-four shift, so his rack will be vacant then. He'll have seniority over the rack because he's ahead in qualification. That means when he wants in, you get out, understand?"

Bill nodded.

"And don't sleep on his sheets. Sleep on top of the plastic flash-cover. It's bunk number twenty-five, third level—that's this level—on the port side, forward, inboard rack on the bottom. There's a small empty locker that's connected to the bottom of rack twenty-seven. It's big enough for two pairs of dungarees and a couple pairs of skivvies—that's all you'll need to bring aboard. If your clothes get dirty, wash them. There's a washer and dryer in the head. Any questions?"

"Yes…uh…how do I…uh…when do I start my qualifications?" The cob opened a small drawer and removed a large card. He handed it to Bill. "This here's your forward qual card. You won't be required to start qualifying until you get off mess-cooking. After that, you'll need two signatures a week to stay even. There's a list of names posted in the crew's mess of who can sign off what. The sooner you start the better off you'll be.

"If you fall behind, you can forget about liberty, and you won't find much time for sleep either.

"We'll be going to sea tomorrow, so there'll be an early breakfast for the men who have to man the steaming watch. Quarters for the liberty sections are at 0630, but that doesn't apply to mess cooks. You'll be expected to report to the cook in the galley at 0430. The yeoman is on liberty, so you won't be able to get a liberty card today. If you want to go onto the beach, just show the tender watch a copy of your orders. I'd better warn you, though, you'll be expected to be on time and ready to work tomorrow—bear that in mind if you decide to go out drinking tonight.

"A couple of other new men reported aboard yesterday. Tomorrow, after the maneuvering watch is secured, there'll be an indoctrination lecture for all of you in the crew's mess. I don't know exactly what time it'll be, but it'll be announced over the M.C. Everything will be explained in detail, and you'll have a chance to ask questions. I guess that's about it for now; you can take off until tomorrow if you like."

Bill looked at the manila envelope he still held in his hands. "What'll I do with this?" he asked.

"The yeoman's office is the first door on the left as you reach the top of the ladder on the first level. Go up the same ladder you came down and keep going around to your left up the second ladder—that leads to the first level. He's not in his office but just leave your records on his desk. I imagine he'll send for you tomorrow to verify your travel allowance."

Bill turned to go. "Thanks," he said.

"Oh, one more thing. If you ever have any legitimate bitches or complaints, or just plain problems, come to me. If you go directly to the wardroom, you might as well piss against the wind. Besides that, you'll be in the shits with me, you understand?"

Bill nodded.

"I don't want to hear any bellyaching though. Don't expect things to be easy around here. If you feel like bellyaching, you better tell it to Jesus, cause if you tell it to me, you'll just get a size nine where it'll do the most good, you understand?"

Bill nodded, and he turned and walked out.

III

There were three parallel passageways in the third level, and three layers of bunks lined the bulkheads in all three. Each group of three bunks was separated from the forward and after groups by thin metal bulkheads extending out the width of the bunks. Each bunk was contained in a small cubicle, just wide enough for one person, and about six feet long and a foot and a half high. Enclosed by green zippered plastic covers, the mattress surfaces completed the containment. On the forward end of the mattress plates, small, riveted, stainless steel squares, with black painted numbers, provided the only contrast to the otherwise identical cubicles.

Bill located his assigned bunk, and he squatted down and examined it. He lifted the mattress and discovered that it just lay on a flat metal bed bottom—no springs.

Fastened to the bottom of the bunk above, he noticed a towel bar, a shoe locker, and another small locker with a door. He assumed that this was the locker the cob had told him about, so he unlatched the door. The locker was small, and he figured that it would be a tight squeeze for his dungarees and skivvies. He wondered what he'd do with his shaving gear.

He reached inside and discovered that it was not completely empty; he pulled out two, obviously used, paperback books. One had its cover completely missing and although the other's cover was intact, its glossy surface was cracked and wrinkled. Staring out from the cover, a girl clad only in black panties and black nylons, stood, with her legs apart, holding two western style pistols. She wore a western hat, which only partially concealed her long, shiny dark hair that flowed down to her bare shoulders. Her breasts were firm and large and two hard-looking nipples pointed straight out in the same direction as the gun muzzles. Someone had drawn a large, black handlebar mustache under her nose and burned a cigarette hole at her crotch. The title of the book, which Bill could make out to be *McCabe's Woman*, had been scribbled over and someone had written *Get Your Gun at Pussy Cultch* in its place.

Bill replaced the books in the locker and stood up. His bunk was among the group that was adjacent to the forward bulkhead of the third level. At the end of the passageway, there was a small door in the center of the bulkhead. There was a window in the door, and he looked through the window at a small area that contained a large green-handled valve, and a number of smaller valves with green and blue handles. It was a non-water-tight, latch-type door, and he noticed that underneath the crack at the bottom, a puddle of water had leaked out into the passageway.

He looked back down at his bunk and sighed. It was a sorry place to call home, he thought. And then he remembered that it wasn't even his. This seemed to be too much to think about, so he tried to put it out of his mind, as he started up to the yeoman's office.

IV

As Bill started up the stairs from the third level, the cob walked out of the chief's quarters. "By the way, Cob, where's the head?" he asked.

The cob pointed forward. "Around the corner and straight…. C'mon, I'd better show you. You'll need to know how to work the valves, anyway."

Bill followed him into the head.

The cob opened the metal door on one of the three stalls. Next to the commode, a large, green, plastic-coated lever stood in an upright position. "This here's the flapper valve," the cob said as he pulled the lever down. Bill watched the flushing hole open and the water drain out. Above the commode, a palm-sized green handled valve stuck out. The cob grabbed the valve and twisted it open. "It's flushed with seawater," he said as Bill watched the water swirl around the bowl and empty into the hole opened by the flapper valve. "All green-handled valves are seawater valves," the cob added, as he twisted the handle shut. Bill remembered the large green-handled valve in the little room by his bunk.

"One thing I want to warn you about. If you ever leave the flushing valve open with the flapper valve shut, it could flood the entire third level. Always make sure the flushing valve is shut tight. The ship's battery is under the desk of the third level, and being an electrician, you ought to know the dangers of seawater leaking on a battery. Not only could it short out the cells, but enough chlorine gas could be released to kill us all."

Bill was still staring at the valves, trying to fix their operation in his memory as the cob turned toward the urinals. "They work the same way," he said, pointing to the green handle of a flapper valve sticking out above one of the three urinals. Oh, another thing, see this red sleeve here—"

Just then, a sailor wearing a guard belt entered the head. "Hey, Cob, Mr. Walker wants to see you. He sure is pissed! I think he wants to know what happened to that supply of foul-weather jackets."

"Goddamnit! I've had it about up to here with that skimmer son-of-a-bitch. What's he doing aboard here anyway? If he'd take his head out of his ass, he'd realize that this is a goddamned submarine, not one of those tin cans he's always talking about. Supply officer! Sheeet! Give one of those flunky J.G.'s a title and right away they think they're important."

"He's up in the wardroom," the sailor said, as he followed the cob down the passageway.

Bill walked over to the center urinal and started unfastening the thirteen buttons that secured the flap on the front of his navy trousers. When his flap was peeled down, he reached in and freed his penis from the confines of his tight jockey shorts.

He closed his eyes and relaxed while a yellow stream of urine shot out and splattered against the urinal bowl. The stream stopped abruptly, however, when he heard a noise to his left, and he opened his eyes to notice another sailor standing before the adjacent urinal unzipping the fly of his dungaree pants. Bill stood motionless, staring straight ahead. He tried, but he was unable to continue pissing. He felt like he was face to face with the enemy with a jammed gun. He hoped that he could stall long enough for the other man to finish, but he must have had to go bad for it seemed that he was never going to quit pissing.

Bill continued to stand there, aimed at the urinal, trying to look casual, as he waited for the other man to go away. The wait seemed forever, and he became embarrassed worrying about whether the other guy would realize that he was becoming embarrassed. Finally, he gave his penis an unnecessary shake and quickly shoved it back into his shorts. The other man finished and flushed his urinal as Bill labored at re-fastening his thirteen buttons. The man was walking out as Bill opened the flushing valve on his urinal. Before he disappeared, the man turned and said, "Just learning, huh?"

His laughter stayed behind as he retreated down the passageway.

Bill wasn't quite sure what he meant, but he understood that he was being made fun of. He still had to go, but he gave up the idea for the time being when he realized how ridiculous he would look if the man came back and caught him doing an act that he had already pretended to finish. He scooped up his records from the sink basin and headed off to find the yeoman's office.

After he had left his records, he started back to the torpedo room to sort out what clothes he would need. As he walked into the crew's mess, the chief was replacing another reel of film on the projector. Bill was halfway through when Parsons called to him, "Hey, C.E., how about pouring me a black and bitter?" Parsons was sitting at the second table from the forward end, over against the wall. He slid his cup down the table and Bill grabbed it.

"Where?"

"Behind you."

He turned around. On the port bulkhead, recessed into the wall, a huge metal coffee pot was mounted on a drain plate. Bill placed the cup under the spout and pulled the plastic handle forward. When he returned the cup to the table, he found another empty one waiting for him.

"Black and bitter," someone said.

Another cup came sliding down. "Blond and sweet for me."

"Start the movie."

The light went out and the projector came on.

"I can't see," Bill protested.

"Stick your thumb over the brim, that way you'll know when it's full."

Bill slammed the cup back down on the table. "Get your own coffee."

"Stop the movie!"

"Huh? What's the matter?"

The lights came back on.

"We can't show a movie when there's a non-qual in here."

"Who?"

Someone pointed at Bill. "Him." Bill wasn't sure, but he suspected that it was the last guy, who shoved him an empty cup.

"You on the list?"

"What list?" Bill asked.

"What's your name?"

"Crazy Eyes Carbary," Parsons shouted out.

Someone got up and looked at the bulletin board on the bulkhead. "Nope, not on the list."

"What list?" Bill repeated.

"The special privileges list. Non-quals can't watch movies unless they're on the list."

"Why are you wasting your time talking to him? He's just a non-qual."

"But I wasn't watching the movie."

"What'd ya say his name was?"

"Crazy Eyes Carbary."

"Gimmie a piece of paper."

"For what?"

"I'm going to put him on my shit list for arguing with a qualified man."

Bill finally caught on to their game. He put his hands together in a mock praying manner. "Oh please, sir," he pleaded, "throw me in the briar patch or molest my mother, anything but that." He stuck his middle finger up and then disappeared through the torpedo room door.

"Hey, Finley, you gonna let him get away with that?"

"Start the movie."

The lights went off.

"Hey, where's my coffee?"

V

Bill sorted out two pairs of dungarees, three pairs of skivvies, three pairs of socks, his shaving gear, a toothbrush, a towel, a washcloth, and a white hat. He relocked his sea-bar, bundled up the gear in his towel, and headed back to his "hot" bunk. The movie was playing when he passed through the crew's mess, so nobody took time to bother with him, and he got through unchallenged.

When he reached the bunk, he crammed his clothes into the locker, hung his towel on the bar, and placed the shaving gear bag at the foot of the bunk. He looked at his watch. It was only three-fifteen. He considered taking the four o'clock liberty launch to the beach, but the thought of being alone didn't appeal to him. He didn't really care for Parsons' ways, but his company was better than nothing. He tried to consider Parsons as a possible friend, but this was hard to imagine. He wondered why Parsons was even bothering with him. Maybe he needed someone to feel superior to? He shook his head. What was the matter with him? This non-qual bit was getting to him already. He felt like a black man in an all-white nudist colony.

He decided to sleep for a few hours, and then get up and go to the beach with Parsons. He removed his neckerchief and hung it on the towel bar, then pulled his jumper over his head.

It felt good to get the hot, heavy woolen jumper off, and he stretched his arms out to enjoy this small sense of freedom. With his arms outstretched, he suddenly became aware of the strong smell of his own body odor, and as he put his arms down, he realized that it was more than just him, the whole third level seemed permeated with the smell of sweat. He reasoned that the smell was probably coming from the numerous sets of dungarees that hung on hooks along the passageway.

It was something he would have to get used to, he thought, as he folded his jumper and placed it next to his shaving gear at the back of the bunk. He wondered how he was going to find a more permanent stowage place for his shaving gear and his blue dress uniform. He thought about asking the cob about it, but then he wondered if the cob might consider that as bellyaching. He remembered what Parsons had said about nobody giving him any slack, and he decided that if he was going to get anywhere, he'd have to be aggressive about it. He accepted that as a kind of resolution and without having decided exactly what action he'd take, he was content to have decided to take some kind of action. He was satisfied to leave any further consideration till some later time.

He swung into the bunk by holding onto the plate across the upper bunk. He lay there for several minutes with his eyes open, just letting his body relax and trying not to think. His mind kept working, though, reminding him of where he was and where he'd be tomorrow. He remembered how he used to think about the coming of a "dreaded tomorrow" when he was back in grade school. It seemed that he had always dreaded going to school in the morning.

He seldom did his assigned homework and feared what the teacher's reaction would be. When he got out of school in the afternoon, though, the next day seemed like an eternity away, and he was always able to put any upcoming unpleasantness out of his mind with the consolation that it was too far away to worry about.

As the yesterdays grew more numerous, however, the tomorrows seemed to arrive more quickly, until finally the thoughts of an unpleasant tomorrow pressed upon his mind. He had come to realize that the tomorrows were inevitable, and that time offered no escapes. He shut his eyes, and he could feel himself falling to sleep. He briefly hoped that he would awake and find it all to be a dream—he still allowed himself some fantasies.

VI

He wasn't sure whether it was the voices that woke him up or the fact that he had to piss so bad. He wondered why he always woke with a hard-on when he had to piss. He looked at his watch. It was almost six. He'd have to wait another two hours. He realized that he probably wouldn't be able to go back to sleep, and he wondered what he'd do with the time. As he lay there trying to find the energy to get up and go to the head, he listened to the voices.

"...Christ, I don't know why this couldn't wait till we get to sea tomorrow. They aren't that full."

"Well, the cob says that the old man wants 'em blown today, and that's it. I think we're going to be playing war games with a couple of tin cans tomorrow, anyway. That's probably why he wants it done today."

Bill could hear a panel being removed from a bulkhead and the clanging of a wrench on metal.

"Maybe so, but I don't see why it has to be done on my watch."

"Oh, you're always bitching. Just blow 'em and get it over with."

Bill finally pulled himself out of the bunk and stumbled toward the head. He didn't notice the below decks watch kneeling at the far end of the head with a flashlight in his hand. Even if he had noticed him, he had to go bad enough so that the presence of someone else would not have stopped him this time. The below decks watch didn't notice him. He had his head in the locker under the sink basins, his attention occupied with monitoring the air gage meter, as he twisted the tan-colored valve handle.

Bill did see the red sleeve on the flapper valve handle over the center urinal, but he didn't know what it meant. And, as he had to piss so bad, he didn't take the time to consider it.

The below decks watch saw him just as he grabbed the valve handle. "Hey! Stop," he shouted.

It was too late.

"WHOOOSSHHH." Brown-colored water, toilet paper, and gobs of shit came flying at Bill all at once. He threw up his hands and leaned backwards. He fell back against one of the commode doors, and the shit followed him. It was like looking at a multi-shaded brown and white kaleidoscope pattern, but these colors really did leap out at him.

Everything but the noisy farting and sputtering shit seemed fixed in a state of slow motion as Bill remained plastered to the commode door and the below decks watch just stared as if in a state of disbelief.

Finally, the below decks watch jumped from his crouched position and slammed the flapper valve shut.

Bill was almost in a state of shock. His face and hair were wet and dripping with brown runny liquid. Across his forehead and down his cheek, a stringy piece of shit paper hung. His wet and splotched T-shirt clung to his body. The doors behind him, the deck, and even the overhead were splattered with shit. He didn't realize it until he was almost through, but the surprise had been too much for his bulging bladder, and drizzling down his leg and over his shoe, yellow urine mingled with the brown puddle of muck that surrounded his feet.

Even the below decks watch didn't escape the surging fluid. He too had been splattered when he jumped for the flapper valve. He shook his arm up and down trying to decontaminate himself. He looked around. "Why does it always have to happen on my watch?" He still hadn't lived down the time he had blown shit up through the captain's washbasin—and now this.

"Wh-what happened?" Bill asked, finally recovering enough to speak.

"You stupid son-of-a-bitch! Didn't you see the red sleeve on the handle?"

"Yeah, but I didn't know what it meant. I've never been on a submarine before."

"That's obvious. You've been to sub school, haven't you? Haven't you ever heard of blowing sanitaries?"

Bill guessed that he must have slept through that lecture, but he said nothing.

Just then, another crew member walked in. He looked at Bill and then at the below decks watch and started laughing. "Goddamn, Gumit! You did it again, didn't you? Goddamn! You're more fun than watching three monkeys fucking a football. Wait will I tell the crew. This is better than an Audie Murphy flick any day. Don't go anywhere." He scampered off.

Gumit looked at Bill. "You better tell them it was your fault."

Bill heard the gob hollering, as he walked toward the head, "Topside just called down and said you're blowing bubbles. When do you think it would be a nice time to secure that—" The cob entered the head.

"Oh! The air!"Gumit said as he hurried back under the basin and twisted the air valve.

"Jesus, Gumit," the cob said as he looked around. "I thought you were qualified."

Gumit was pointing at Bill. "He...he...."

"Did you have the secured chain hooked across the head door," the cob patiently asked.

"Well...I had the sleeve on the flapper valve!"

The cob started to say something else but stopped. He shook his head. "I hope you two have a nice time cleaning this mess up." He turned around and pushed his way out from the crowd of men who were starting to gather at the head door.

"The non-qual's got an excuse for being dumb. What's your excuse, Gumit?"

"Don't ask him hard questions, you'll embarrass him."

"Remember the time he left the tools in the washer and someone turned it on?"

Everyone laughed.

"How come you're always in the shits, Gumit?"

[More laughter.]

"Hey, non-qual, when I said you were on the shit list, I didn't think you'd try to commit suicide."

Bill knew that they were bound to get around to him.

"I wonder if he opened his mouth in surprise?"

"Smile, C.E.," Parsons said. "Let's see if you have brown teeth.

"We can't leave the head without tracking this shit all over,"Gumit said. "So, why don't one of you apes make yourself useful and go to get a bundle of rags?"

Someone went to get the rags and the crowd gradually broke up.

Bill removed his T-shirt and stood in front of a mirror picking strands of toilet paper out or his hair.

"Don't worry, it won't leave any marks,"Gumit said. "But there might as well be." He nodded toward the door. "They'll never let you forget it, you know."

Bill noticed that Gumit had warmed up somewhat. In a way, Bill was glad to have been included in the ridicule.

"How come they jumped all over you? They didn't know what happened."

"Don't kid yourself. They knew what happened all right. One look at you doesn't leave much doubt. But what happened has nothing to do with it. The opportunity was there and that was all that was necessary. You can't let it get to you. Next time the shoe might be on the other foot and you can laugh."

"Well, I don't think it's right to laugh at other people's mistakes."

"Right? The next time you see someone covered with shit, you remind yourself that it isn't right to laugh. What'd ya mean by 'right,' anyway? Don't go trying to apply your church style morals to this world. It's different. You don't know yet, but it's different from civilian life. It's even different from the ordinary Navy, it's…it's…."

…almost alive, Bill thought. He remembered those opaque eyes and wondered if he could change enough to understand.

"One thing—I've never seen anyone make the same mistake twice."

Bill felt defensive. "Maybe so, but I don't see why everyone feels that it's necessary to be rough on someone just because he's a non-qual."

"Well, I don't suppose that many people really stop to think about it. They just take it as the way to act in the world we live in. But there's a reason behind it—it makes a man want to get qualified, if for no other reason than to get out from uncer the screws."

"I think encouragement would work just as well."

"Yeah, well maybe. But I'll tell ya one thing. Encouragement alone wouldn't get rid of the deadwood. Ya gotta prove you can take it to be part of it. You know what I mean?"

The man came back with the bundle of rags and threw them at Gumit.

"Hey, Granny, wait a minute,"Gumit said as he set the bundle down on the sink basin. He took his guard belt off and threw it at Granny. "I have to clean this mess up, take a shower, and put on clean dungarees. You got the load for about an hour. I'll relieve you early off your watch, tonight. Everything's normal except that we're charging H.P. air on number one air tank. The clipboard's up in the crew's mess on the chief's table.

"You forgot one thing," Granny said.

"What's that?"

"Sanitaries have been blown!" Granny walked away laughing.

Chapter III

Silver Dolphins on her chest
She's been had by the navy's best
One hundred men she'll thrash today
But only three in the normal way

—Radio station S.T.U.D.

I

As the liberty launch pulled away from the tender, Parsons licked his finger and held it up to the wind. "Yup, wind's coming from port. Hey, C.E., would you mind moving starboard?"

"How about taking a flying leap at a rolling doughnut?" Bill said.

"Did you used to say that in high school, C.E.? That's clever. Did you hear that, Dingle? The non-qual's being insolent. Write that down."

Dingle whipped out a pen from his jumper pocket and started writing on the palm of his hand.

"Oh, Christ," Parsons said. "They ought to make you an officer. Gimme that pen." He grabbed the pen from Dingle. "Here, keep it in your pants," he said as he shoved the pen into dingle's trouser pocket.

"Hell, two beers and he can't even keep his pants," the other sailor said.

"You nukes are all alike," Dingle said. "You flap your jaws a lot, but that's all you know how to do. I'll outdrink any one of you."

"We'll see, we'll see," Parsons said.

"Hey, Dingle, show the non-qual your tattoos." The other sailor said.

Dingle unbuttoned his sleeve and pushed it up past a snake until the arm of a hinge could be seen extending out from the underside of his elbow joint.

"He's even got a spider web on the back of his elbow," Parsons added. "But that's not his neatest tattoo. C'mon, Dingle, show us your special tattoo."

"Go to hell."

"He's got a tattoo on the head of his dick," the other sailor told Bill.

"Aw, you're kidding."

"Wanna bet? He's got a rosy pair of lips tattooed around the …uh…mouth."

"It's more like a nose," Parsons said, "the way it was running a few months back."

"Dingle caught a 'cold' down in T.J. a few months ago," the other sailor said. "When you were… uh...cleaning the head today, did you notice the bent flushing pipe over the center urinal? Dingle did that the first time he tried to take a piss after his 'cold' revealed itself."

"Yeah, and if that wasn't bad enough," Parsons added, "The doctor on the tender wanted to write him up because of his tattoo. Even called up the old man. What was it he told him, Garcia? Something about never having seen such a gross example of stupidity. The skipper sure got a kick out of that."

"You should have had an eyeball tattooed there," Garcia said, "then maybe you could've seen your way to avoid those contagious crevices."

"It could've happened to anybody," Dingle snorted. "Tell us about the last time you went to T.J., Garcia."

"He had to beg the price of a phone call from some skimmer, so he could call up the boat for someone to come and get him," Parsons said.

"Did you spend all your money?" Bill asked.

"Nope," Dingle said. "He got rolled."

"But you're a...."

"You ever see a Mexican blush?" Parsons asked.

Garcia changed the subject. "We still want to see your tattoo, Dingle."

"He will show it to us when he gets drunk. He always does." Parsons started laughing. "Were you there, Garcia, the time the barmaid in the Brown Bottle chased him out into the street with a butcher knife. She said she was going to cut it off. Would've too, if she'd caught him. I never saw Dingle run so fast in all my life. The next day he had wind burn on his foreskin."

I'll never believe that," Dingle said. I think you guys made that up as a joke."

"Dingle forgets when he gets really drunk," Parsons said.

"I can understand that," Garcia said. "How else could he live with himself?"

"I'm not so sure he forgot that incident, though," Parsons said. "How come you never go into the Brown Bottle anymore, Dingle?"

"You guys can laugh now," Dingle said, "but when I carry you all back to the boat, we'll see who laughs last."

"Aw shit, Dingle, I bet the non-qual can drink more than you can."

II

The liberty launch pulled up to the float alongside of the pier and Parsons jumped out, "Hand me your sea bag, C.E.," he said.

Bill handed him the bag and then stepped over on to the float.

Parsons handed the bag back to Bill and then they all stepped from the float on to the pier. They walked without talking down the pier to the large parking lot filled with cars belonging to various crew members. As the four men walked across the parking lot, they passed a girl who was heading toward the sub pier. A blue suit dress clung tightly to a shapely body and the slightly undersized matching top buttoned some of the bounce out of her bulging breasts. Pinned to her suit top and perched on top of her right breast, a pair of small silver dolphins jiggled and gleamed in the sunlight as her long legs carried her quickly and deliberately away from the four men who had stopped and were staring after her.

"Boy, I'd eat that for breakfast," Dingle said.

"You wouldn't know what to do with it," Parsons said. "You torpedo men are all alike. You have no finesse. Take my advice. Stick to whores, and leave the delicate work to us technicians."

"Aw, Christ," Dingle said. "You'd probably spend all day looking for the fine adjust knob while I'd be running hot, straight, and deep."

You always think of things in terms of torpedoes, don't you? I think you're sick, Dingle. I bet you'd paint rosy lips on the head of all the war-shots if you thought the old man would let you get away with it."

"How come she was wearing dolphins?" Bill asked.

"She's probably the wife of a qualified sub-sailor," Parsons said.

"A lot of the wives wear dolphins."

"Yeah, either that or she fit on the entire crew of one of the boats," Garcia added. "That's how Snorkel Patty qualified for hers."

"Who's she?" Bill asked.

"She can't be described," Parsons said. "She has to be experienced. You haven't lived until you've had one of her hot water hummers."

III

Bill thumped his sea bag down on the gravel driveway between two of the barracks-style buildings. "I gotta rest a while," he said. "How about one of you guys carrying this for a while?"

"You can handle it, C.E.," Parsons said. "Besides, there's only a little way to go."

"Well, do what you want, but I'm going to rest." Bill looked around. "What are these building here for anyway?"

"All the other boats are allotted barracks here," Parsons said. "We haven't had any since I've been aboard, though."

"That's because the cob never gets off his ass and does anything for us," Garcia said.

"It's because these goddamned nukes are never in port long enough to rate barracks." Dingle said. "It isn't like this on the old boats."

"What do you know about the old boats?" Garcia asked. "I didn't see any dolphins on your chest when you first came aboard. I bet you were never on an old boat."

"Well, I was," Parsons said. "I spent my first two years on the Runner, and I'll tell you for a fact that we put in many months at sea in the North Atlantic. I remember one time when we were coming back in port after making a Med-cruise. We'd been gone seven months. There were wives and kids and girlfriends all standing on the pier waiting. We were close enough to see them. All the line handlers and everyone else who wasn't doing anything was up topside rubbing their dicks and—"

"They were what?" Garcia asked.

"Well, maybe they weren't doing that, but they were excited. After all, it had been seven months—"

"Who are you shitting, Parsons?" Dingle asked. "You can't tell us you made a Med-cruise on one of the old boats, and you never hit port. I bet you half the crew had the clap."

"You're an expert on that, aren't you, Dingle?" Garcia asked.

"That and torpedoes," Parsons added. He pulled a couple of cigars from Dingle's jumper pocket. "Ya ever notice how he always carries around cigars? Never smokes them. Just looks at them and strokes his fingers over them every once in a while. You're sick, Dingle."

Dingle grabbed the cigars. "Gimme those. And stop trying to get off the subject. How many ports did you hit?"

"Well, yeah, we did hit a few ports, but that's another story. Anyway, there we were—"

"And that's the difference between the old boats and the nukes," Dingle interrupted. "The nukes go out for months at a time and then return back to the same place. They never hit any liberty ports. Anyway, go on."

"I forgot where I was."

"You were up topside playing with yourself," Garcia said.

Parsons waved his hand limply at Garcia. "Oh, you are the gross," he lisped. "Anyway, there we were, only about ten minutes from mooring, when the

captain gets a message from squadron, and we turned around and headed back to sea. Some fisherman spotted what he thought was a Russian submarine, and we spent the next four days out there looking for it.

"I tell you, when that boat turned around, a couple of sailors had to be restrained from jumping overboard and swimming for shore. And if you think it was hard on the sailors, you should have seen the wives. I heard they just about tore apart the squadron office. Of course, they wouldn't tel them why we left, where we were going, or how long we'd be gone. All's they would say was that the wives would be *notified*." Parsons shook his head. "Boy, talk about some angry women. One guy's old lady was so pissed-off at the navy and her husband because he was in it, that she went out and fit on the first guy that would have her. It broke up the marriage when her old man found out."

"Didn't you used to be married, Parsons?" Dingle asked.

Bill was looking at Parsons's face, and he saw the small lines that appeared only for a moment at the corners of his eyes. No one else noticed.

"Yeah, I made that mistake once," Parsons said. "But my wife wasn't on the pier that day if that's what you're insinuating. She was back in Arkansas living with my parents. As a matter of fact, I thought the situation was rather funny. It didn't bother me that we were going back to sea for a while, and I got kind of a kick out of hearing everyone pissing and moaning."

"You sure have a warped sense of humor," Garcia said.

"Yeah, well, war's hell." Parsons pointed at one of the buildings further down the driveway. "Over there's the locker club, C.E. You can drop your gear off and meet us at the Pump Room." He pointed again. "It's the building right across the way." He laughed. "Don't take too long or you'll miss the great scene when Dingle dangles."

IV

Bill dragged his bag up the steps of the locker club and opened the door. He held the door open with one hand and, with his free hand and his foot, he boosted the bag over the door sill and followed it inside. Once inside, he leaned against the wooden ledge extending out from the window cage and stared at the man sitting inside the cage area.

The man's knees were bent, and his legs were folded back underneath the chair that was propped back on its two rear legs. His belly was enormous, and it rivaled his head as the highest point of the teetering heap as it pushed against the buttons that fastened his dungaree shirt.

Standing upright on top of his stomach, a paperback book acted as the joining strap-buckle that connected his circular arms and, in a comical sense, seemed to be holding him down. The man's eyes were focused on the book and Bill hadn't noticed that he hadn't even looked up when he entered. He assumed that he must have heard him, though, so he stood leaning on the window ledge waiting for some response. Finally, the man turned a page of the book.

"Uh… excuse me," Bill said.

The man looked around and then up at Bill. "Why, you do something?"

"I'd like a locker."

"Ya got an I.D. card?"

Bill smiled. "Yeah." He made no move to reach for his wallet; he just stood looking at the man waiting for him to ask for it.

"That's nice," the man said as he leaned back in his chair and started reading his book again.

Bill considered leaving, but the thought of hiring a taxi to haul him and his sea bag all the way downtown didn't appeal to him. He pulled out his wallet and placed the card on the ledge. "Here it is."

The man leaned forward again and picked up the card. He opened a file drawer and started thumbing through the cards.

"Ya ever have a locker here before?"

"No."

"What ship you on?"

"The Sculpin."

He slammed the file drawer shut. "You didn't come here looking for trouble, did you?"

"Look, all I want is to rent a locker. That's what you're here for, isn't it?" Bill looked at him intently. "You got a boss?"

"Alright, alright. How long do you want to rent it for?"

"I dunno. A couple of months, at least."

"That will be $33.39."

"You gotta be kidding. What for?"

"If you're on the Sculpin, you know that it's going on a West-Pac in three weeks and won't be back for six months. That's six months in advance; take it or leave it."

V

When Bill entered the Pump Room, he immediately saw Grade and Dingle playing pool in the center of the room. Father back in a corner, he located Parsons sitting at a table. As he walked over, he noticed Parsons was motioning to the bartender. Bill pulled up a chair and sat down, and Parsons reached up and snatched the hat off his head.

"Don't you know better than to wear a cover in a barroom?"

"Yeah, yeah, I just wasn't thinking. That locker club guy pissed me off so much—"

"Got to you, huh? Figured he would."

"You figured…?" What'd ya mean? What's the deal anyway?" Bill stared at Parsons. "Did you set me up?"

The bartender came over and set down a pitcher of beer.

"Pay the man, C.E.," Parsons said. "It's your turn."

Bill pulled out a dollar and some change and slapped it on the table. The bartender picked the money up and left.

"Now that's what I mean, Parsons. You did it to me again, didn't you? How could it have been my turn? I know damned well you guys haven't drunk three pitchers of beer already. And even if you had, it wouldn't make any difference. I wasn't even here."

Parsons laughed. "Don't get all worked up, now. The only person that did you was yourself. Why'd you pay for it if you didn't want to? But you're right; we aren't taking turns. This is our second pitcher; we flipped for both. Parsons shrugged. "You lost both times. I got generous, though, and bought the first one anyway. I don't know what's getting into me." He laughed again.

Parsons's cackling laugh was starting to grind on Bill's nerves. "You sound like a hyena," he said.

"Thank you."

"Whaddaya know about that locker club creep. He got something against guys off the Sculpin?"

"Yeah, he's one of those guys who can't take a joke. One of our sonar men—they call him Lurch. I don't even know what his real name is. You will know why they call him that when you see him—he's about six-four and in the neighborhood of two-fifty. Anyway, Lurch swatted him once, a couple of weeks back. He was just having fun with him, you understand, and the guy almost landed inside one of the lockers, which wouldn't have been so remarkable except that the door wasn't open."

Parsons poured Bill and himself a glass of beer. "Anyway, like I said, the guy couldn't take a joke, and he took the whole thing personally. Not that he said anymore to Lurch, though. He went up and bitched to squadron. Actually wrote Lurch up for striking a senior petty officer or something like that. Those skimmers are all alike.

"So, squadron sends a couple of shore patrol down to notify the old man. The skipper told them he'd take care of it and the shore patrol left. The old man already knew about it, because Lurch and the two other guys who were there had already told Mr. Lawson how this guy was wising-off, and how Lurch was only funning with him, and then Mr. Lawson told the captain.

"The old man got a big laugh out of the whole thing and Lurch was back onto the beach the same night. Now, Lurch is a pretty easy-going guy, but when he found out about that skimmer going bellyaching to squadron, well, that did get to him a little. Not that he was mad enough to hurt anyone, but he did want to let the guy know he was pissed." Parsons took a drink of beer, shook his head, and started laughing. "I wish I would have been there."

"What happened?"

"Well, he went over there and walked into his little office— didn't say a word—just picked the guy up and carried him outside. And that guy isn't very light; you've seen him. Lurch had him slung over his shoulder, and he was flailing and hollering. It didn't do him any good, though. Lurch still stuffed him into the dumpster. Well, I'll tell you one thing, the guy didn't go bitching to squadron about that. He hasn't smartened up much, though. Every time he can get away with it, he gives someone from the Sculpin a hard time. He'll probably keep it up until someone else slaps a knot in the side of his head. What'd he say to you, anyway?"

"Nothing much. He just charged me six months in advance. How come you didn't warn me about that guy?"

"Look, don't blame me if you can't take care of yourself. How come he wanted six months in advance?"

"And that's another thing. You've could've told me we were going on a West-Pac in three weeks."

"You never asked."

"Well, that's why he wanted it, because we're going to be gone for six months."

Garcia and Dingle came back to the table and sat down. Dingle grabbed the pitcher of beer and filled up both their glasses.

"How come you let him do you like that?"

"Whaddaya mean?"

"He fit you on. You didn't have to pay six months in advance. You could have paid a couple weeks locker rent and then put your gear in storage while we're in West-Pac. It shouldn't've cost more than five or six dollars."

"Well, how am I supposed to know? You could have told me these things before."

Parsons laughed. "How you over gonna learn to get along on your own if someone always looks out for you? Now take the Mexican, here." Parsons motioned with his hand toward Garcia. "Garcia's our after-minority representative. Our forward representative's name is Dories. He's a Guamanian pineapple. Anyway, Garcia occupies an important position back aft. Someone has to be inferior, and he handles the job quite well.

Doesn't bitch or ask for any help either. They were going to send a black dude, but they couldn't find one that could make it through nuke school. The wetback here, slipped right through, though. What I can't understand, though, is that since it's a Spook's billet, how come they didn't send two Mexicans?"

"I can't understand why someone hasn't punched you out," Bill said.

"Why should anyone do that? Maybe I do bend people a little but it's all for their own good. Someone is going to do it sooner or later, and I figure it's better for me to do it first, because I don't mean 'em any harm. Then, when they do run up against someone who really leans on 'em, they're not so apt to break."

Bill took a drink of beer. "You really believe you're doing people a favor, don't you?"

"I try to do what I can."

Bill stared at Parsons, wondering if he was really serious. He decided that in his own way he was. "Anyone ever get to you?" he asked.

"Some try," Parsons said," but no one can do the impossible."

Parsons erupted into his cackling laugh, but Bill continued to stare. "Maybe they just don't know where you live," he said.

VI

"Let's play puddles," Dingle said as he poured a puddle of beer on the table.

"Funny," Parsons said staring into his beer glass, "I didn't love her when I married her, but I did when I divorced her."

Dingle started thumping in the puddle like he was playing a tom-tom.

"Christ," Parsons said, shielding his face with his hand. "Cut it out, will you? You're getting me wet. Besides, you'll wake up Garcia."

Dingle settled his hands flat on the table and then dragged them back toward his body trailing his fingers through the puddle. Beer drizzled down to his lap, as he folded his palms over the edge of the table and rested his chin on his fingers. "Ya wanna see my tattoo?" he asked.

"I've seen it," Parsons said.

He turned to Bill. "Ya wanna see my tattoo?"

"Not now," Bill said, "some other time."

Dingle flopped his arms on the table and settled his head on his forearms. "Goddamned non-qual," he said.

Bill picked up his glass and sloshed the little bit of beer around that was in the bottom. He shook his head. "I don't know why I drink this stuff, I don't really like it."

"Well, Garcia offered you some of that tequila."

"That would have been all I needed. I feel fuzzy enough as it is. What time's it getting to be, anyway?"

"Don't sweat it, we got a while yet before this place closes. You wanna see a picture of my little girl?" He reached for his wallet.

"Sure. I didn't know you had a little girl. How come you got married anyway? I mean you said you didn't love her."

"Not when I first married her, no. Here, look, she was two when this picture was taken. But she'd do anything for me. You know, she really loved me. And I did like her. Who needs love? I wasn't even sure what it was. Whaddaya think of my kid? She won a photo contest with that picture."

"She's really cute. I can see why you're proud of her. But what happened, I mean with the marriage?"

Parsons put his wallet back in his pocket. He took a deep breath and released it. "It was a marriage, that's what happened. They change after you marry 'em. I'll never get married again. And, after the kid came, things were really different. Not that I'm blaming Lauri. Christ, I love that kid. It just kills me to be split apart from her.

"Anyway, after Lauri came, it seemed that me and Jodi were fighting all the time. She sure had some strange ideas. I remember one time I came back home in the afternoon after being at sea for two weeks. I wanted to take her to bed, but she didn't think it was right to do it in the daytime. And besides the kid was up. Can you imagine that? The kid was only one year old. Anyway, she locked herself in the bedroom, and I ended up kicking in the door. She was the only woman I ever raped."

"Did it do any good?"

Parsons laughed. "It did me some good. I don't know what it did for her. She didn't talk to me for three days. She finally broke down when she realized that I wasn't letting it get to me. I'll tell you one thing; she never locked me out of the bedroom again."

"So, what finally happened? I mean to finish it."

"Well, last year when I can back off a patrol, she told me she'd filed for a divorce."

"That's too bad."

"That's what I figured. I wasn't about to let her get a divorce out here in California. Do you realize how much they soak you for out here?"

Bill shrugged. "What could you do about it?"

"I sweet-talked her out of it. She always was soft for sweet-talk. That's one thing she was always bitching about—that I never talked nice to her. Well, I finally did, and I hope she learned a lesson from it. She probably didn't, though; she never had too much common sense."

"But if you talked her out of it. How come you still got a divorce?"

"Because as soon as I got her to withdraw the papers, I took emergency leave and flew back to Arkansas and filed. She never contested. Never even showed up in court. I could have gotten away without paying anything, but I agreed to fifty dollars a month, so I could get to see my kid."

"But you said you loved her. How come you divorced her?"

"Because she tried to do me."

Bill finished the beer that was in his glass, replaced the glass on the table, and watched the bubbles setting back to the bottom. He rested his elbow on the table and propped his forehead against the palm of his hand. "It's been a long day," he said. "And what am I doing here?" He shoved the glass away from him. "I don't even like the shitting stuff."

Parsons laughed. "You said that before."

Bill shook his head. "It always gives me a headache. Yet I've been sitting here for hours drinking it. I even paid for most of it."

He looked up at Parsons. "You are a son-of-a-bitch, you know that?"

"Thank you."

"How do you know I won't do you?"

"You're alright, Bill."

"What's that supposed to mean? And how come you're calling me Bill? You've got the whole boat calling me "Crazy Eyes," and now you've decided to call me Bill!"

Bill settled back in his chair and stared at Parsons. He still had the same self-assured smirk on his face, but Bill could see through it now, and it no longer irritated him. He looked at Garcia and Dingle and then back at Parsons. He realized that they were going to be friends, and it bothered him a little that he had been chosen instead of having done the choosing. But in a way, he was also flattered.

"I don't even know your first name."

"Frank."

Bill smiled. "Fuck you, Frank," he said.

VII

Bill took a sip of the hot, black coffee. "Christ, I've been on this boat less than twenty-four hours, and it seems like I've spent half my time lugging things up and down that tender ladder."

Parsons laughed. "Did you notice the look on the watch's face when Dingle leaned over the rail and started making those weird noises like his guts were coming out?"

"Yeah, he didn't even want to see his I.D. card. All he wanted was for us to get him out of there."

"Too bad he only had the dry heaves."

"At that point, I don't see how he could have had anything else. He left a trail in the water all the way from the pier. At least he could walk by himself, though. Garcia kept passing out every five seconds. He would have fallen all the way from the top of the ladder if I hadn't been behind him to hold him up."

"That's what I like about the guys here," Parsons said, "they know how to have a good time."

"Getting a little drunk is okay, but I think that's going a little too far."

"Well, consider yourself lucky, then. You could have been just like them. Garcia wanted to pour some of that tequila into your beer when you were in the head, but I stopped him."

"Kind of out of character for you, isn't it?"

"Well, maybe, but I was thinking ahead. I wasn't about to saddle myself with three drunks to carry back to the boat."

Bill looked at the clock on the bulkhead. "Christ, it's two-thirty already. I'm supposed to report for mess-cooking at four-thirty. I'm going to be dead on my ass tomorrow. How do I go about getting up then, anyway?"

Parsons yawned. "You put a call in with the below decks watch. I wouldn't worry about it if I were you, though; you are really not going to be mess-cooking."

"Whaddaya talking about?"

"You ever wonder why you got assigned to a boat when most of the other guys from your class got tin-cans and carriers?"

"Well, I was at the top of my class."

"That's one of the reasons, but that alone wouldn't have gotten you here. Unlike most of the other nuke boats, we happen to be hurting for electricians. We just lost three of them. One got out, one got kicked off the boat, and one made warrant officer. We did have a surplus of electricians, but all at once we're short, and that's where you come in."

"But the cob said—"

"Yeah, well the cob just don't have his facts straight. And unlike the old boats, the cob is not really in charge of *all* the enlisted men. Oh, technically he is, but the nukes kind of go their own way. Maybe you've noticed already that there's a little friction between the nukes and the noseconers. It pisses some of the noseconers off that we get pro-pay, and they don't. Anyway, what it all boils down to is that the engineer—that's Mr. Browder—is the big daddy of all the nukes, and since he's a lieutenant commander and the cob is only a chief, he has just a little bit more horsepower."

But if the engineer wants me back aft, how come the cob doesn't know about it?"

"I don't know. Maybe he does, or maybe the engineer didn't feel like lowering himself enough to discuss it. He's like that. At any rate, you can count on one thing—there's going to be a flap over it. You'll be going back aft though. Browder may be a prick, but he does stick by his men."

"So, what do you think I ought to do? Report for mess-cooking or forget about it?"

"Well, I'm sure the engineer's back aft, because they're doing a cold-water light off. You could try going back there and kind of stand around until he notices you. I wouldn't bother him unless he speaks to you first, though. He's kind of high-strung and the least little thing—especially when he's involved in a critical operation like this light off—will send him into spastics." Parsons laughed. "Hell, just last month, he kicked Chief Mitchell in the shin because there was a low-level alarm on one of the surge tanks.

"On second thought, though, maybe you'd better not go back there. If he notices you've been drinking, that'll really set him off. He's been really uptight about drunks back aft ever since Wensel came back plowed to the gills and dropped a monkey wrench in the back of one of the switchboards.

"I was on watch at the time. I could see the sparks all the way from the maneuvering room. Tripped every breaker in the main power line. Luckily, I was able to reclose the starboard MG-AC breaker and restore vital power from the battery. That really could have developed into an incident if we had been critical. As it was, Browder had to call Admiral Rickover and explain what happened. Wensel, by the way, got demoted to fireman and shipped to a tin can. That is, after he got out of the hospital—singed all the hair off the right side of his head, even his right eyebrow. Luckily, he came away with his eyesight. He was a good man too, just couldn't hold his booze. I think he did it on purpose."

"Why?"

"Because he wanted off. He put in a non-vol chit, but they just ignored it." Parsons shrugged. "So, he threw a wrench in the switchboard—he was just trying to get their attention."

"You sure it wasn't an accident? Seems like a pretty dangerous thing to do on purpose."

"Well, he should have known better, if that's what you mean. Said he used the wrench to unfasten the cover plate nuts, and he was performing a semi-annual P.M. (preventive maintenance) cleaning the dust out of the board. I'll say one thing for him, if there was any dust in there, he sure got rid of it.

"But like I said, I don't figure it was an accident. Even as drunk as he was, he was still an electrician, and he knew better than to mess with an energized switchboard with an uninsulated wrench. Besides, you're supposed to get the captain's permission to work on an energized board. That's what they got him on—failure to follow regulations. There was talk that they just wanted to get rid of him with as little mess as possible."

"Why did he want off, anyway? Everyone told me the subs were pretty good duty."

"The old boats are. And even the nukes aren't bad duty for the noseconers. But the guys back aft really take it in the ass. Hell, us R.O.s (reactor operators) have been on port and starboard for over a month—that's duty every other day and six on and six off when we're at sea. And when these things go to sea on patrol, you can forget about getting letters or communicating in any way with anyone in the real world. You won't even see daylight or breathe fresh air for more than two months. It's hard on everyone, but it's worse on the married guys. There were *six* divorces after the last run we made."

Bill could see the tension in Parsons's face, and he realized that he was feeling bitter about his divorce. "How long you been aboard?" he asked.

"Two years. I just got a set of orders for instructor duty at a "C" school here in San Dago, but the bastards cancelled them. Put an operational hold on me till we get back from West-Pac. By that time, I won't have enough time left to rate shore duty, and I'll be dammed if I'll ship over. It's like a mouse trap—they lure you in with sweet-smelling bait, and then, once you're inside, the bait turns to shit, and the trap springs, and it won't loosen up until it squeezes the life out of you."

Bill smiled. "You're not letting them get to you, are you?"

"You mean because I bitch little? Listen, sometimes you come up against things that you can't do anything about. Then you have to find ways to live with it. My way is bitching. You'll have to discover your own way. The people who let things get to them are the ones who throw monkey wrenches in switchboards."

"Well, maybe so, but I was just wondering if you were bitching or crying?"

Parsons laughed. "You're alright, Bill."

Bill got up. I'm going to bed. Whoever wants me in the morning can come get me."

"You say that very loud and the whole crew will be lined up in front of your bunk."

"I guess I'll see you tomorrow. Maybe then you'll have better control of yourself."

"Whaddaya mean?"

"Look at all the information you volunteered tonight."

"Yeah?"

"Well, I didn't ask." Bill headed down to the third level.

Chapter IV

Oh, it's hard, ain't it hard, ain't it hard
To leave your love and then go out to sea
Well, it's hard, ain't it hard, ain't it hard…
GREAT GOD!
To stay out there and never to be free

—Radio Station S.T.U.D.

I

Bill opened his eyes for only an instant when the small bag thudded against his feet at the foot of the bunk. Had he been awake enough and taken the time to think about it, he probably would have realized that the owner of the bag also owned the bunk. The man walked away, however, and it was sleep not distance that first separated Bill from his departing footsteps.

"All hands man the maneuvering watch," a voice crackled over the MC speaker.

Bill opened his eyes.

"Man the maneuvering watch," the voice repeated.

Bill closed his eyes and pressed in on his eyeballs with his right thumb and forefinger. Then he remembered. He groaned

58

and rolled out of the bunk onto his hands and knees in the passageway. He jumped to his feet immediately when he felt the cold puddle of water on his bare knees. He stood with his head down and his arms outstretched with his hands grasping on to the metal plate of the opposite top bunk. Water drops from his knees drizzled down his shins and were absorbed by the tops of his socks which were already soaked on the bottoms from standing in the puddle.

His head hurt, his mouth was dry, and a lingering rotten taste reminded him of all he had to drink the night before. He looked at his blue uniform, which he had hung on one of the hooks. The trousers were hung first, and the jumper was humped over them. One of the sleeves folded up inside itself so that just a few inches stuck straight out from the shoulder. The other sleeve hung limply and Bill noticed the discolored chunky smear where he had rubbed against the railing that Dingle had barfed all over. He remembered that he had not yet found a place to keep his dress uniform. He left it where it was and removed a clean dungaree uniform from his tightly packed locker.

II

Bill started up the ladder to the first level but stepped back down when he noticed that someone was coming down. "Hi, Cob," he said as the Cob squeezed past him and continued around the corner down toward the third level. Bill stared after him and wondered why he hadn't answered.

After he reached the top of the ladder, Bill stood staring at the closed watertight door that separated the forward end of the ship from the after engineering spaces. He wanted to go aft but he wasn't sure what "manning the maneuvering watch" involved, and he was afraid he would be breaking watertight integrity if he opened the door. He stood undecided for a few moments and finally turned with the intention of going down to the crew's mess when he heard the door unlatch. A sailor stepped through, and Bill stepped up and grabbed the latch handle before the man could swing the door shut. He shoved the door back open and ducked through the oval opening.

He closed the door behind him and, for once, he looked upon surroundings that did not appear totally unfamiliar. He was in what he knew to be the reactor compartment tunnel, a narrow, shielded passageway that stretched along the top of the reactor compartment. Bill found a certain solace in seeing things that he recognized from his training at the prototype. He couldn't help mentally testing his memory, as his gaze shifted from one component to the next. Cooling pipes, valves, air cylinders, tanks, gages, and meters all leaped out and were translated from their outward independence to a more interconnected, unified meaning. But, things were not complete, as his memory was imperfect, and some things were different, and somethings were altogether new. He realized that if he was to become useful, he would not only have to become an interconnecting operator of the various systems, but he would also have to become a functioning unit in a larger system—the submarine. And, as he surveyed the working guts of the whale that had swallowed him, he realized that it would be a mountainous task.

"Now shifting main coolant pumps to fast speed," came a voice from the MC speaker.

Bill heard the giant, remote-controlled breakers slamming shut in the adjacent compartment.

"Main coolant pumps one, two, three, and four are in fast speed," the MC voice said.

Just then, a sailor, carrying a pencil and clipboard, walked in from the after compartment.

Bill watched him as he recorded gage readings at the after end of the tunnel. When he had finished there, he moved forward to the center of the tunnel and started into the RC through the thick glass windows. He continued to stare for an unusual length of time, and then he looked up at Bill who had been standing watching him.

"Can't make it out," he said. "Can you read that water level?"

Bill looked through the window. "What water level?"

"The steam gen—" He shook his head. "Never mind." He gave Bill a look of disgust and stared again through the window. He scribbled something on the clipboard and then shifted over to the window on the opposite side.

Bill continued through the tunnel into the next compartment.

III

In the center of the upper level auxiliary machinery space ("AMS"), two parallel rows of switchboards provided the prominent furnishings. There were five boards in each row, each measuring about six and a half feet high and three feet wide. The switchboard faced outboard, and a narrow passageway separated the two rows and provided a straight path from the tunnel to the engine room door.

Bill didn't stop in the AMS to look around but, instead, proceeded directly into the engine room. He did notice the group of men who were sitting by the workbench in the after starboard corner of the AMS, but he hesitated only long enough to be sure that there was no familiar face among them. Once inside the engine room door, he quickly stepped aside for a chief who was coming through.

The chief straddled the door opening and shouted into the AMS. "How about a couple of you guys giving us a hard with these shore power cables?"

He then ducked back into the engine room and Bill had to step aside again, as he squeezed past and climbed up several rungs on the after-hatch ladder.

"C'mon, c'mon, lower that goddamned cofferdam (an aluminum three-piece structure that attaches to the outer hatch of a submarine and is used to keep the shore power cables elevated and away from the water).They're waiting on us!"

One section of the bulky aluminum cofferdam came clanking down through the escape trunk, and the chief grabbed it and, without even turning around, he lowered it down with one hand and swung it out toward Bill. Bill automatically grabbed it, set it on the deck, and looked again just in time to be ready for the next section which was being passed down to him. By the time the third section came down, two more men were standing alongside of him.

"Heads up," the chief said as the heavy brass cap, dangling by a chain from the head of a shore power plug, bounced off the top rung of the ladder and swung into the air.

The cable was being lowered by a rope and the chief guided it down into the hands of the men waiting below. The long black cable was as big around as a fence post, and it took all four men to ease it down and snake it out on the deck. After the second cable was lowered, Bill got out of the way as the electricians up above passed their tools below and then, one by one, stepped backwards down through the escape trunk hatch and into the engine room. The last man to come below pulled the outer hatch shut after him and cranked the wheel that dogged it tight.

Next, the lower hatch was shut and dogged.

Bill stood in the main passageway waiting for a chance to look into the open doorway of the maneuvering room that was now blocked by a sailor who was leaning over a chain hooked across the opening. Several times Bill had to turn sideways to make room for passing sailors. Their criticizing glances made it obvious that he was considered an obstruction to the smooth flow of things. He finally moved deeper into the engine room, finding a small corner next to the big still where he could be out of the way and yet see into the maneuvering room just across the passageway. The sailor had not moved from the doorway, however, and Bill could only see the top of someone's head over the man's hunched shoulders. He turned his attention elsewhere.

Overhead, huge padded steam pipes only somewhat muffled the roar of the high-pressure steam that was pouring into two giant constant-speed turbine generators occupying the whole center area of the upper level engine room. Farther back, an even larger turbine unit provided twisting power to a strong steel pillar-like shaft that connected to an external propeller-shaped screw. The power link was broken now by the disconnected clutch, and the turbines whirled against little resistance, as the operator at the secondary throttle station *warmed up the mains* by spinning the throttle wheel first in one direction and then in the other. The racing blades on the turbine wheels alternately wound up to a screaming pitch and then slowed down to a whisper.

Aside from the main engines, though, the engine room noises were fairly constant, and they were such a familiar part of the background that the watch standers noticed them only if they stopped.

When Bill again looked towards the maneuvering room, the sailor was gone, and he could finally see into the "heart' of the engineering spaces. Just inside the doorway, the steam plant control panel (SPCP) operator stood before the primary throttle control station. Behind him stood a sailor with a headset on.

Further on, in the center of the room, Parsons sat facing the reactor plant control panel (RPCP) with his hand on the rod control lever. Bill knew that there was an electric plant control panel (EPCP) operator outboard of Parsons, but his line of sight was blocked by the other watch standers, and he could only see one arm casually draped over the chromed support bar that ran along the lower edge of the three panels. Behind the dungaree-clad watch standers, an officer, wearing a khaki uniform, sat in an elevated chair. Bill assumed that he was the engineer.

"The mains have been warned," the upper-level watch said, poking his head into maneuvering.

"Very well," the officer said. "Shift control to the SPCP."

"Shift control to the SPCP, aye." The upper-level watch headed back toward the secondary throttle station.

Shortly, he returned to maneuvering. "Control has been shifted, sir."

"Very well. SPCP, check for control in the ahead and the astern direction."

"Check for control in the ahead and astern direction, aye." The operator spun open and shut the large throttle wheel and then did the same with the smaller one. Each time, the needle of the smaller R.P.M indicator gage jumped up to about fifty.

"I have control in the ahead and astern direction, sir."

"Very well. Request permission from the bridge to test the shaft on the EPM (emergency propulsion motor)."

"Request permission to test the shaft on the EPM, aye." The phone talker pushed down the button on the mouthpiece. "Bridge, Maneuvering, request permission to test the shaft on the EPM." A brief pause and then he depressed the button again. "Maneuvering, aye, Bridge." He turned toward the officer. "Test the shaft on the EPM."

And with what might seem, to an uninitiated observer, like a reversal of roles, the officer repeated, "Test the shaft on the EPM, aye." He picked up the 2MC microphone, and his voice bellowed out over the engineering spaces, "AEA (auxiliary electrician aft), report to Maneuvering."

A sailor stepped through the engine room door from the AMS, and Bill noticed that it was the same man who had previously blocked his view. He stuck his head into maneuvering. "Test the shaft on the EPM," the officer said.

"Test the shaft on the EPM, aye," the sailor said as he started aft.

After a short while, Bill noticed the needle of the large R.P.M. indicator gauge jump to about 5 R.P.M.

Bill heard the AEA's voice coming from the X60J speaker. "Maneuvering, AEA, shaft tested on the EPM in the ahead and astern direction; test satisfactory. Permission to engage the clutch?"

The officer removed a handset from the phone holder by his head. "AEA, Maneuvering, engage the clutch."

"Engage the clutch, aye."

A red light went out on the SPCP and a green light came on. The SPCP operator turned toward the officer. "Clutch indicates engaged, sir."

"Very well."

"Clutch indicates engaged, Maneuvering," a voice came from the speaker.

"Maneuvering, aye, AEA," the hidden EPCP operator answered.

"Test the shaft from the SPCP."

"Test the shaft from the SPCP, aye."

Again, the operator opened the large throttle wheel, but this time his actions were very precise and deliberate. He watched the large R.P.M indicator intently, and as soon as it first started to move, he shut the throttle. He did the same with the small throttle wheel, only this time he watched for the red light, and as soon as it came on, he quickly shut the astern throttle. The operator turned toward the officer. "Shaft tested, test sat," he said.

The officer stared at him. His words were emphatic and clipped when he replied. "Shaft tested in the ahead and astern direction, test satisfactory, aye." He turned toward the phone talker.

"Report to the bridge that the shaft has been tested and that the engineering spaces are ready to get underway."

The phone talker pressed down the button. "Bridge, Maneuvering. Shaft has been tested; the engineering spaces are ready to get underway."

IV

"Your name Carbary?"

Bill turned toward the chief whom he had helped with the shore power cables. "Yeah. You the chief electrician?"

"That's right." He held out his hand. "Name's Tanner. We've been expecting you. The yeomen told us you'd be here this week. C'mon into the AMS where we can talk."

Bill shook his hand and then followed him into the AMS. There was a group of men still gathered in the corner. The chief stooped next to these men and leaned against the metal workbench at the after end of the compartment.

"You missed muster this morning, you know."

"Yeah, I…uh…overslept."

"Yeah, well that happens occasionally, I guess." The chief stared at him. "About once every five years. Right? Anyway, no harm really done. Parsons told me you were aboard. He had trouble getting up this morning too. He was a half hour late in relieving the watch. That's a bad habit to get into. Tends to piss people off. Anyway, nobody's going to get down on you for just one time. You understand what I mean?"

"Yeah, you don't want me to do it again."

"Right. And if you got a little hangover in the morning, well, I can understand that too. Don't expect any extra consideration if something needs to be done, though. The cob was back here a little while ago. He's not as understanding as I am. I'd stay away from him for a while. He's out to chew ass, and he didn't get any satisfaction from the engineer."

"What'd he say?"

"Oh, nothing much. Didn't get a chance. We've been pretty busy back here with this light-off and all. Browder didn't want to bother with him. He just told him what was what and that was it. Parsons stuck up for you about not reporting for mess-cooking, so you're safe there. Like I said, though, I'd watch myself for a while. It's not good to get too well known, too soon. But the cob isn't the type to hold a grudge, so don't let it bother you."

Bill shrugged. "I just take things as they come."

"That's good because we got a battery charge coming this afternoon and you and one of the other off-watch electricians are going to take gravities (a method of measuring the degree of charge of a wet-storage cell-type battery). You ever take gravities before?"

"No."

"Well, now's a good time to learn. I'll send Grimshaw down with you. He'll show you how. You got an old pair of dungarees?"

"No, I only brought two new sets aboard."

"Well, you'll have an old pair by the time we get back in."

He pointed to a book stuck in a metal pocket screwed to the back of one of the switchboards. See that EDOI (engineering department operating instructions) over there?"

"Yeah."

"Well, sometime today—before sixteen hundred—I want you to read the procedure for going into the battery well. Make sure you know it. You might as well read about the different kind of charges while you're at it. You'll have to learn it sooner or later, might as well be now."

Just then, Bill felt the ship move, and he braced himself against the bench for support.

Tanner laughed. "It will seem strange for a while, but you'll get used to it. I understand the seas are pretty rough today, and it will be a while till we go under, so I want you and Gibson to go down into the lower level AMS and secure any loose gear." He looked over at the group of men. "You get that, Gibson?"

"Goddamnit," Gibson mumbled. "I knew if he saw me sitting around here, he'd think up something for me to do."

"Whaddaya say, Hoot?"

"Yeah, I got that, Chief."

Gibson got up and walked over to the lower level AMS hatch and started down. Bill started to follow him. He walked a little unsteadily, because the ship was now moving slightly from side to side.

"And Carbary, one more thing."

"Yeah, Chief?"

"After you get done there, see Chief Palmer about getting an after-qual card. Then you can start qualifying. Oh, you will be on AEA training watches with Gibson. He has the 12 to 4s."

"Where do I find Palmer?"

"He'll be around. He's kind of rotund, has dark curly hair, and a hooked nose. He looks like a Jewish Winnie the Pooh." Tanner laughed. "Oh, and see the Yeoman sometime today."

"Yeah, okay, Chief." Bill grabbed hold of the AMS deck hatch cover and steadied himself, as he stepped down onto the ladder.

V

"Goddamnit! Goddamnit!" Haden kicked the refer-compressor. "They are always thinking up some kind of busywork. I must have been out of my mind to volunteer for this duty. It's like volunteering for a kick in the ass. And I even extended for pro-pay. Shit!" He kicked the compressor again. "Ya know what the 'pro' stands for? Prostitution, that's what. Bodies! That's all—just warm bodies to do busywork."

Bill was sitting on the elevated step leading up to the main coolant charging station. His head was lowered, and his hands covered his eyes and enveloped his forehead. His elbows were propped on his knees. The sub was slowly rolling from port to starboard and then back again. He could hear the water in the bilge beneath his feet, as it came splashing up and then sloshed back down again. Bright green circles of color appeared and disappeared on the back side of his closed eyelids. His stomach churned and occasionally forced up a burp with some terrible-tasting slime. The first time it happened, Bill tried to spit it out, but it wouldn't break off, and it swung back onto his chin and then onto his shirt when the ship rolled back to starboard again. After that, he swallowed the slime back down, and it made him sicker each time he did it. He could hear Haden talking but he tried not to listen. "Oh, Christ," he said shaking his head slowly.

Haden kicked the diesel engine this time. "I ought to tell them. I ought to walk right up to—hell! to the old man! [Haden laughed.]I'd say, 'Pete'—I'd call him—'Pete'—that'd fry him—I'd say, 'Pete, jam this busywork right up your ass!'"

"Oh, Christ."

Haden picked up a green oxygen candle canister. "I'll stow his gear." He shoved the canister behind the electrostatic precipitator (electrical filter for removing particles of dust from the air). "He can jam this up his ass, too. This goddamned boat sucks!"

"Oh, Christ."

"This goddamned navy sucks!"

"Oh, Christ."

"The whole goddamned world sucks!"

Bill started barfing in the bilge.

Haden watched him for a moment and then moved around to the other side of the diesel and started stowing gear.

VI

The door on the yeoman's office was divided into two sections so that the top half opened independently of the bottom half. The top half was open, and Bill leaned over the bottom section. The yeoman was inside the small office, typing. "You wanted to see me?" Bill asked.

The yeoman looked up. "Dunno. Who are you?"

"Carbary."

"Yeah, yeah, just a minute." He started typing again. Finally, he finished and, as he pulled the paper from the typewriter, he looked back up at Bill. "You wanna extend another year?"

"What for?"

"For pro-pay, idiot! It's hard to understand, but that's the money they pay you nukes because you're so smart."

"Yeah, I forgot." Bill put his hand to his brow and wiped the sweat off his forehead. "I don't feel very good."

The yeoman stuck a card in the typewriter and started typing again. "You don't look very good. You look kind of green. Didn't you ask the doc for a sea-sick pill?"

"Where can I find him?"

"They won't do you any good now." He pulled the card from the typewriter. "We should be under in about a half hour. That should help." He handed the card to Bill. "This here's your liberty card. Sign here, and don't lose it."

Bill signed the card. "Thanks" he said.

The yeoman pulled a piece of paper from a shelf. "How'd you get here?" he asked.

Bill looked at him blankly. "Uh… I just walked back from the A.M.S."

"Jesus, another one! The boat's already full of them and we get another one. Listen, Dumbo. How—did—you—travel—to—this—duty—station? Did you fly in an airplane (the Yeoman flapped his arms), or did you drive in a car (he held his arms outstretched in front of him and moved his fists up and down)?

"Oh—I flew."

"Now, one more thing, do you want to extend?—that means sign up for another year."

"Let me think about it. I'll let you know."

"Yeah, sure." The yeoman turned back to his typewriter and inserted another piece of paper.

As Bill walked away, he could just make out the Yeoman's grumble above the clatter of the typewriter keys, "Goddamned nukes!"

VII

Gibson was sitting back on the electrician's bench looking at a log sheet when Bill came back for his training watch. "Well, here I am," he said.

Gibson looked up. "Whoopee. What are you doing here so early? You didn't eat first call, did you? Trainees are supposed to eat second call."

"No, I didn't eat at all. My stomach's still a little unsettled."

"Yeah, well, that reminds me, when you get a chance, you can hose down the bilge area around the charging station."

"Okay. Where's the hose at?"

"I'll show you later. Right now, you have to learn how to take readings so next hour you can do it on your own."

"Alright, I'm ready."

Gibson looked at his watch. "Don't be so eager. It's not time yet. We got two more minutes." He picked up a card from the bench and handed it to Bill. "Here, Chief Palmer gave me this to give to you."

Bill took the qual card and looked at it. "Boy, they sure load it on you all at once, don't they?"

"Yeah, some more than others."

"Whaddaya mean?"

"Well, I just moved up one notch from the bottom of the S.L.J. list when you came aboard."

"What's S.L.J. mean?"

"Shitty little jobs."

"Well, someone's got to do them, I suppose."

"Boy, you're a regular philosopher, aren't you? You might not feel so understanding when you get out of the battery well this evening. You ought to be finished in time to get at least two hours sleep before you have to come back on watch at midnight. How much sleep did you get last night?"

"Not much, but that was my own fault. What does 'D.C. Aft' mean, anyhow?"

"What're ya talking about?"

"Up on the watch quarter and station bill. They got me down for D.C. aft for battle stations."

"Oh, that's 'damage control, aft'! That means you come back here in the AMS during battle stations and stand by. I'm D.C. aft, too. Where've they got you for maneuvering watch?"

"Shore power."

"Yeah, well that's hard to get away from, being an electrician. You'll love it when we come into port, and we're still hooking up shore power while everyone else is going onto the beach."

Just then, the e-call growler squealed, and Gibson reached over and grabbed the handset mounted on the bulkhead.

"AMS Gibson speaking."

(Pause)

"Yeah, yeah, I was just going in."

(Pause)

"Alright, I'll send Carbary up." He shoved the phone back in the bracket.

"Jesus, you'd think the world was going to come to an end if you're one minute late taking your goddamned readings. And they want more coffee, too. That's one thing I hate about this watch—you have to wait on those prima donnas in maneuvering. I never should have relieved Niles without checking the coffee jug. Well, you'll have to take it forward and fill it up from the big coffee pot in the crew's mess. It's in the engine room mounted on the big still. I'll have to show you how to take readings next hour."

VIII

The cook stuck his head out of the galley door and shouted at Bill, as he stood before the big coffee pot, unscrewing the lid of the jug. "Whaddaya want? What're ya doing? You can't take all the coffee. This is chow time. Don't you nukes know anything? You're not supposed to come up for coffee during chow time."

Bill looked at the glass indicator tube, and without looking up at the cook, he set the jug lid on the drain plate and started filling the jug. "You got plenty," he said. "It's almost full."

One of the sailors sitting at the outboard side of the table next to Bill reached over and goosed him.

"Ouch!" Bill jumped, and coffee drizzled down the side of the jug and onto the deck.

"You better clean that up, nuke," the cook said.

"He's probably too good for that, Cookie," another sailor said. "He's even too good to be a mess cook."

Unnoticed by Bill, the sailor who had goosed him reached over and removed the jug cover from the drain plate. He passed it to the man next to him, and it was quickly relayed into a bulk-head locker.

"You mean he's the guy who brown-nosed his way out of mess-cooking?" the cook asked. "You won't last very long on this ship, Nuke. I'll remember you when you come to me for a checkout on this compartment—if you're around that long." The cook reached into the galley and found a rag. He threw it at Bill. "Here, clean up your mess before you leave."

Bill finished filling the jug and reached for the cover. He turned around. "Alright, where is it?"

"Where's what?"

"They put it in that locker over there," one of the men at a back table said.

"You nukes stick together, don't you?"

"You going to give it to me?"

"Get hosed, Nuke."

Bill picked up the rag from the floor and tossed it at the sailor who had goosed him. "You caused the mess, you clean it up," he said. He turned and headed back aft with his uncovered coffee jug.

About five minutes later, Bill was smiling when he returned to the crew's mess carrying a flashlight and a red tag. He calmly walked over to the lighting panel on the forward bulkhead and opened it up. All at once, the lights went out.

Two battle lanterns came on, but they only dimly lit the large eating area.

"Hey, what happened?"

"What's going on? Call maneuvering. Did they lose the T.G.s?"

The cook came hurrying out of the galley carrying a flashlight. "What happened to our lights? Did someone call maneuvering? What's going on back there? I didn't hear any alarms."

"That was no accident. Lighting's on the vital bus. Someone must have turned them off. Check the lighting panel."

"No need," Bill said. "I turned them off."

"Well, turn them back on."

"Get hosed," Bill said.

"Someone turn those lights back on," the cook said. "You're never going to get it back now, Nuke."

"Get what back? I'm just looking for a ground." Bill turned toward the man who was opening the lighting panel. "There's a red tag on that lighting breaker. Signed by the engineer. You wouldn't want to violate a red tag, would you?"

"There is a red tag here," the man said.

"You can't detect a ground on lighting from back aft," someone said. "Lighting power goes through transformers."

"Just doing my job," Bill said. "There is a ground in here alright, and I think it's in that light right there." Bill shined his flashlight up at a lighting fixture over the center table. He squeezed in between the men and stepped up between two men on the bench.

"Hey, get out of here! What're ya doin'?"

Bill pulled a screwdriver from his pocket. "It'll just take a minute. Could someone hold my light, please?"

"Hey, get off me! Fuck your light."

"It'd be easier if I could stand on the table. Could you move those plates?"

Most of the men in the room were laughing. The others were just staring.

"What are you letting him do that to you for?" the cook said. "Get him out of there."

Bill was unfastening a screw.

"Hey, you're getting dust on me. Jesus, someone give him back his jug cover."

"What cover?" Bill asked. "I'm just doing my job."

"Here's your cover, now quit messing around up there and turn the lights back on."

Bill took the cover and refastened the loose screws. "I think I fixed it," he said.

"Well, turn the goddamned lights back on."

Bill jumped down and started aft. "Can't, he said. I have to get the engineer's permission to clear a red tag. We'll call you when it's okay."

IX

"C'mon Bill, wake up, wake up." The voice kept filtering through into Bill's consciousness. He resisted it and turned over. A hand came in and shook his shoulder. "Wake up Bill, it's me."

Bill shoved the hand away. "Who are you? Go away. The chief said I could sleep in until the maneuvering watch."

"C'mon Bill. It's me, Frank."

"Frank? Whaddaya want? Leave me alone."

"C'mon, get up and have a drink with me—I got a bottle."

Bill stuck his head out and looked at Parsons. "A drink? You're crazy." He looked at his watch. "Christ, we'll be in in about four hours. Can't you wait?"

"Why wait? I want a drink now. Besides, I have duty when we get in." He pulled Bill's dungarees off the hook and threw them at him. "Here, get your clothes on and let's go down to the storeroom."

Bill pulled himself out of the bunk, put his clothes on, and followed Parsons down to the storeroom. They sat down on a couple of five-gallon soap cans and Parsons reached behind one of them and pulled out a bottle of bourbon.

Bill held the cups while Parsons pored. "Go easy on mine," he said. "Jesus, I don't know why I let you talk me into this. This was the first chance I've had to really sleep since we left port. It's always been something. The first two days I hardly slept at all. And since then, I haven't been able to spend two straight hours in the rack without something waking me up.

"Christ, they got me up to qualify; they wake me up to attend lectures; they have battle station twice a day—and they always pick my sack time; and if that isn't enough, when I do get to sleep, one of these tin cans would come along and drop PDCs (practice depth charge—small exploding devices with about the same explosive power as a hand grenade)."

Parsons set the bottle back down behind the boxes, reached over, and gave a cup to Bill. "Have a drink; it'll make you feel better."

"And now you. Couldn't you find someone else to drink with you?"

"Yeah, sure. But I wanted someone to shoot the shit with, and I just happened to think of you. Besides, you like it and you know it; you wouldn't be here if you didn't."

Bill took a drink, sloshed the bourbon around in his cup, and then looked up at Parsons. "Like what? What are you talking about?"

"Oh, there's a lot of crap to it. And it gets most of us down. But there's something more. It's hard to label or put your finger on, but it's there, and I think you know it—you're becoming part of it. I knew you would. Some never do."

"Yeah, I think I know what you mean." Bill put the cup to his lips, tilted it up, and then, without allowing any liquid to enter his mouth, he moved it away. It wasn't a pretending gesture; he had just changed his mind. "I wonder...." He shifted his gaze from the cup, which he supported in front of his face, to Parsons. "I wonder if it's not just a mutually shared fantasy or if there's anything real to it."

Parsons took a long drink and then put his cup back down on his knees. A smile appeared and quickly vanished. He looked at Bill. "So, what is real?"

Chapter V

As each day passes, some
Of us are different than
Before
Some of us are less of
What we were and some of
Us are more
And all of us are some
Of both, but none of us
Are sure
That what we are and what
We'll be are better than before
And a few of us observe the pain,
But most of us ignore
And some of us move quietly
And some of us, we roar

—Liam

I

The barroom was dark but not as dark as it had first appeared when Bill had stepped in out of the sunlight. The music from the jukebox was loud, and the hard rock background beat pounded in rhythm to Bill's tapping finger. Only occasionally did the lyrics filter through into his consciousness and invite his thought-voice to join in and temporarily push aside the wandering thoughts that were filling in the slowly passing seconds. His mind was not totally involved in other things or other places, however; he was painfully aware of where he was and that the short glass of beer that he grasped firmly as if for support was his ticket of pretense.

He had gotten off for liberty at nine o'clock and, as he had nowhere else to go and no one to go with, he had boarded a bus that had taken him to downtown San Diego. There, he had wandered the streets for about an hour, stoically resisting the sidewalk pitchmen who tried to lure him into their jewelry stores or encyclopedia parlors. Now and then, he would wander into a Go-Go bar, but drinks were expensive, the pool-playing sailors offered no companionship, and the time that was used up seemed surprisingly little.

He refused to play the flashing, clanging machines in the penny arcades—partly because this seemed a juvenile form of entertainment, but mostly because he refused to show any kinship to the other sidewalk wanderers, who, both uninformed and not, displayed a seemingly embarrassing amount of frivolity that appeared foreign to a hot mid-day downtown street. Inwardly, he envied them, not because he thought they were enjoying themselves, but because they were not alone, and they at least appeared to have something to do. But Bill gave no outward thought to this emotion. He considered them as "skimmers" or boots, and he consciously worried that someone might regard him in the same way.

He kept an eye out for familiar faces, optimistically hoping that he might see someone from the sub. He knew that this was highly unlikely, though, as the guys off the boat were not the same kind of sailors that he passed on the San Diego streets. He remembered about the hangouts that he had heard some of the guys talk about, and it was those remembered stories that had caused him to board the bus for Ocean Beach.

Ocean Beach was a beach-town suburb of San Diego. There was a beach, many small houses, a small business district, and bars and taverns. The beer palaces catered largely to the sailors who made up a sizable proportion of Ocean Beach's transient inhabitants.

Bill was impressed immediately that Ocean Beach was markedly different from San Diego. A person could feel less aware of himself and his surroundings in such a place. Oh, there were still sailors to be seen on Ocean Beach's streets— hardly ever in uniform, though—but they didn't seem without a purpose, or at least they appeared casual enough so that a purpose didn't matter.

But Bill was unable to lapse completely into the carefree atmosphere. And, as he sat in the Brown Jug tavern, holding firmly onto his purported purpose for being there, he wondered if he'd find a worthwhile, or at least a diverting, way to pass his free time, and he wondered if he'd ever fit in.

Above the bar, he noticed pictures of different submarines. He picked out the Sculpin, and he tried to imagine himself as being within that dark, gray, semi-submerged tube that was caught in a frozen state of suggested motion. It seemed unreal.

He wondered just why he was where he was—not just in the bar, but in his entire present situation in life: being where he was, who he was, and thinking the way he did. When he was a young boy, he used to think that of all the many people that he knew to be in the world, there must be someone just like him. Now, he no longer felt that way. There were too many things that changed a person. Too many things happened because of whimsical choice, many unforeseeable things happened, and many things chosen cleared a strange pathway. Bill felt that there were many men within a man and which personality dominates the surface indicates who a person is but not necessarily who he was or will be.

He didn't believe in determined destination. His pessimistic and lonely current-representing self, mused that the only thing man was destined to be was a fool, with only the degree of foolishness being variable—according to will, chance, and interpretation. Bill didn't know what he'd be like tomorrow; he only knew that he was changing, and that he was a different person than he was yesterday.

He looked again at the submarine picture, and he thought about the enchantment he had associated with submarines as an adolescent. Perhaps it was all the World War II submarine movies that he had so avidly gobbled up. Or maybe it was the publicity that the advent of the nuclear submarine had thrown at him. He laughed. Or perhaps it was a Freudian urge that had decided his path. A return to the womb, maybe? He took a drink of beer and shook his head…or a search for the tomb?

The sounds and sights of the bar lost their clarity as his conscious-directed thoughts gave way to remembering and gradually the remembering was replaced by re-experiencing.

* * *

"Bill—eeee," his mother shouted.

Bill heard her, but he didn't answer. He was around the back of the house lying on the slanted wooden cellar door. The door had absorbed the heat from the noonday sun, and it felt good on his back, as Bill stared up at the fluffy drifting overhead clouds. He liked to watch the clouds. He would imagine that they were animals or other things. If he couldn't think of anything that a cloud looked like, he would make up something. It just couldn't be nothing, he reasoned. It had to be something. Everything had to do or be something.

"Bill—eeee."

Why wouldn't she give up? He couldn't go in now. He had wet his pants earlier, and he was waiting for them to dry. Why'd she always bother him? She hardly ever bothered Terry.

Terry had gone off to play baseball. Bill's father had once made Terry take Bill along—but no more. "He'd just get hurt again," Terry had protested, and besides, he's no good. He can't hit, and he can't catch."

And that was all right with Bill. He didn't want to play baseball with Terry or his friends. They always threw the ball too fast, and they were never nice to him. They would always argue which team would have to take him, and he would always end up on Terry's team because he was his brother. And they would call him "cross eyes."

His eyes weren't really crossed, though; only one eye would focus, while the other eye drifted to the outside. Bill wasn't to know till years later, but it was the resulting lack of depth perception that had contributed to his poor baseball abilities.

"Bill! Didn't you hear me calling for you?"

"I was just going to come."

"Well, you come on right now. Your grandfather's here." His mother turned and walked back to the front of the house.

Bill jumped up and followed his mother. He loved his mother's father. He seemed to have an understanding and a genuine appreciation of Bill's personality that his other relatives lacked. It wasn't that the other relatives weren't nice to him, they just considered him as being somewhat different.

"How come Bill spends so much time by himself?" his aunt had once questioned.

Bill had overhead that conversation, and he understood that maybe it was bad that he liked being by himself. What they said wasn't going to change him, though, he wasn't going to be like Terry, and they couldn't make him.

Inside, his Grandfather was sitting in the large overstuffed chair talking to Bill's father. Bill ran in and hopped up on the chair's arm. He hugged his Grandfather around the neck and the old man slipped his large hairy forearm around Bill's waist. "How's m' boy?" was the old man's characteristic greeting.

He was a large man, a former logger, who, in his sixties, still did strenuous physical labor, and although he had spread out in the middle, a tightened fist would cause cords of muscle to bulge out on his beefy forearms. Bill would often run his fingers through the old man's steel-gray hair or feel his leathery cheek, which was usually roughened by a day-old growth of whiskers.

His breath often stank of beer, and he generally wore only a t-shirt in the house, even during the colder months. His daughters would nag him about his drinking and his appearance, but they didn't have the influence that his departed wife once did, and he paid them no mind. Like his appearance, the old man's manner was rough, but Bill could always tell that his heart was kind, and he never mistook his coarseness for harshness.

He had been blessed with seven daughters, and although, or perhaps because, he had no sons, he had very strong ideas on how a young boy should be raised.

And, as he sat shaking his large knuckled fist under Bill's nose, the young boy's fist under his own nose was an indication that his methods reaped, from Bill at least, both appreciation and response.

Bill was plainly the old man's favorite. He seldom bothered with Terry anymore. He had been rebuffed many times by the older boy who had never understood the old man's ways. Terry was much closer to his own father whose gentle-harsh nature was softened more toward his first son than his second.

"Cry uncle, cry uncle!" the old man shouted as he tickled Bill's ribs.

Bill wiggled and squirmed, and through his giggling laughter he blurted, "No fair! No fair!" as he tried in turn to tickle his grandfather. As the old man continued to tickle Bill, he threw his head back and laughed loudly; it wasn't because Bill was tickling him, though, the old man was pleased that Bill was a fighter and that he never tried to escape or run away.

When Bill discovered that tickling did no good, he reached up and grabbed his grandfather's thick gray hair and pulled as hard as he could.

The old man let out another burst of loud laughter, although the lines on his face indicated that he felt the pressure of Bill's strong grip. "Oh, m' boy, so that's your game, huh?" He reached down, grabbed a handful of Bill's hair, and pulled with ever-increasing pressure. "Cry uncle, Bill. Cry uncle." (He never called the boy "Billy" as his daughter did.)

Bill's head was forced back against his shoulders and his mouth, clamped shut, stretched across his face in a thin line, which parted only slightly displaying the white of his clenched teeth.

His eyes were squinted shut and, at one of the corners, a tear was squeezed out and rolled down his check. It wasn't a tear of despair or anguish but a tear of determination that was forced out by the tremendous screwed-up effort that Bill exerted against the pressure that was pulling at his hair roots.

"Give up? Cry uncle?" his grandfather asked, himself slightly wincing from the surprisingly strong pull that Bill still exerted on his own hair.

"Stop it, Dad. Stop it!" Bill's mother screamed, having falsely interpreted the boy's tear.

The old man let go but Bill held on firmly and demanded an "uncle."

"Uncle, uncle," the old man said throwing up his hands, inwardly discovering a sense of relief that his daughter had ended an uncompromisable contest.

"You are tougher than I figured," Bill's father said as he leaned over and slapped him on the leg. He quickly drew his hand away, however, and stood up towering over him. "Did you piss your pants again!" he shouted more as an accusation than a question.

Bill lowered his head. He didn't have to look at his father to know that his face was red, and his eyes were staring hard and cold.

"You are seven years old. Why do you act like a baby?" He took off his belt. "Well, I'm going to give you a lesson to remember."

Bill's mother stepped in between. "Bill, go to your room. Lee put that away. The boy can't help it."

"He can't help it? Don't give me that shit. It's time he started acting his age. You baby him too much, that's the problem."

In his room, Bill covered his head with a pillow, but he could still hear the shouting, and he could hear the front door shut when his grandfather left. He never cried "uncle," but in his room alone, Bill often cried.

II

"You want another one?"

Bill focused his eyes on the barmaid who was standing in front of him. He released his grip on the empty glass and nodded his head. "Yeah, sure," he said. He looked around the barroom. At the far end of the bar, two half-empty beer glasses awaited a couple who shuffled around out next to the pool table. The jukebox blared a pounding rhythm, which seemed to provide only an excuse not a purpose for the tall, big-bellied man to move awkwardly back and forth while clutching and maneuvering a much smaller, younger, seemingly listless partner. Somehow, the scene looked grotesque. They were moving too slow to be dancing to the music, and even so, to Bill, dancing seemed strangely out of place in an almost empty tavern in the middle of the day.

Bill looked away from the couple, but soon found himself looking back. The girl's arms hung loosely to her sides, but the big arms of the man were wrapped around her in bear-hug style, and Bill envisioned a rag-doll being slowly squeezed and swayed to and fro by a giant unintelligent dough-man.

The side of the girl's face pressed into the puffy chest, and the long brown mousey hair hung straight down with no hint of a curl. The face was not unattractive, but sewn into the rag-doll appearance was a pitiful, terribly lonely, but also resolved expression.

Most men would have noticed no more than two people dancing and thought no more about it. But Bill, especially Bill, could see more. What he saw seemed somehow unreal. Sometimes, he experienced feelings of being separated from himself, with only his physical self being a part of the world he was looking at. He felt that way now, and it was an unsettling feeling. He quickly shook his head and looked elsewhere.

Behind him, a long, shiny shuffleboard stretched parallel to the bar. It had been the stories that he had heard about the Brown Jug and what had happened on that shuffleboard court that had caused him to pick this tavern. The story had seemed quite funny when he had first heard it back on the boat—but now, as he looked at the shuffleboard court, he could no longer rekindle the humor. It wasn't that he became disgusted by the thoughts of what he'd heard; he admitted to himself that if he heard the story again in the same context, he would probably find it to be equally as humorous. But in the bar, all alone, and in his present mood, the vision of two sailors eating out the barmaid on the shuffleboard court didn't even cause him to smile.

Gabby had said that the barmaid's name was Dolly. He glanced to his left at the barmaid and considered calling her by that name and then thought better of it. He turned to look at the dancers again and was somewhat startled to see the girl occupying the seat next to him.

He stared at the girl only for an instant. She didn't look at him. Her head was facing straight ahead and was lowered slightly. Her hands were entwined in front of her on the bar. Although he couldn't see her face directly, Bill sensed that she had the same tragic look on her face. He glanced over her head down the bar. The dough-man stood up next to the bar staring at him or at least staring in his direction.

The barmaid sat on a stool at the entrance end of the bar with her chin propped up by an elbow supported arm. Apparently, she was listening to the now surprisingly soft music, or perhaps she was just off in another world like Bill himself often was.

Everything seemed frozen, except for second hand of the clock that kept slowly moving around. Bill could hear his heartbeat. He considered ordering another beer for himself or maybe the girl, or perhaps even thumping his fingers up and down on the bar—anything to break the continuous state of unchanging noises, which seemed no different than silence.

He did nothing. The clock's second hand progressed for another ten seconds—it seemed like ten minutes. He thought about just getting up and leaving, but he made no move to do so. Finally, as he stared across the bar into the mirror on the opposite wall, he accepted what had shaken him so much about the girl's appearance—it was the complete picture of tragic loneliness that he had observed traces of in so many faces, and which was now mirrored back at him in h s own face. He put his hand gently on the girl's arm and she turned toward him, seemingly unsurprised by his gesture. "C'mon, let's go," he said softly.

III

Once out in the diverting openness of the bright noisy street, the spell was broken, Bill's thoughts were no longer freed to honesty and, as he looked at the meek pale girl who still clung onto his hand, he was struck immediately by the unfamiliar strangeness of his present situation. He started walking up the street; the girl started to follow but she stopped.

"My-my pills," she said.

Bill looked at her.

"He has my pills. I'm an epileptic."

Without even thinking about what he was saving or why, Bill looked back toward the tavern and said, "I'll get them."

She dropped his hand and looked down toward the sidewalk. "You don't have to," she said softly. "He won't give them to you."

Bill didn't say anything else. He thought to himself that the whole situation should be funny or ridiculous or perhaps even stupid, but it was only a passing thought, and it didn't really bother him as he walked back into the darkness.

As he stood just inside the barroom, waiting for his eyes to readjust, he listened to the barmaid who stood opposite across the bar talking on the phone.

"—yes, First and Pacific. He seems to be bleeding pretty bad. You'd better hurry." She hung up the phone and looked at Bill. "Look, fella, we're going to be closed up for a while. Some crazy guy just put his fist through the juke box glass." She walked down to the center of the bar and started washing glasses. "Boy, we get them all," she mumbled.

He looked down toward the far end of the barroom. There, sitting on the floor with his head buried into his knees, the dough-man sat with a blood-soaked towel coiled around his right hand.

Bill turned and walked back out to the street. He half expected and perhaps even hoped that the girl would be gone, but she wasn't. "You have any more pills?" he asked as he took her hand and led her down the street.

IV

"Papa Joe's Pizza Parlor" seemed in a way like the San Diego penny arcades. It wasn't open ended, but it was obvious and phony and, although the clanging bells were missing, long bright fluorescence tubes stretched along the overhead and illuminated the numerous mid-afternoon haven seekers with their "combination" pizzas and light and dark beers. A cylinder-operated player-piano jukebox clanged out a "Gay Nineties'" tune and the warped cylinder produced what seemed to be both a comical and appropriate effect.

Bill had passed this place on his way to the Brown Jug. He hadn't given it much thought at the time, but after leaving the tavern with the girl, he had come directly here. Drinking beer always either made him hungry or gave him a headache, and he reasoned that if he went somewhere where he could eat and have another beer at the same time, he could stall off the headache a while longer. He felt a little juvenile and foolish bringing the girl into a pizza parlor, but he would have felt even more foolish had he given in to his original inclinations—an afternoon movie and a stroll on the beach.

The girl had said she wasn't hungry and ordered only coffee, and although Bill offered her several wedges of his "pie," she stoically refused.

"How come you were with that goon, anyway?" Bill asked. He inwardly winced at the stupidity of that question. He was always doing things like that—being overly aware of what he was thinking and then talking like a fool anyway. He hadn't even asked her name. He felt that he had waited too long and now he didn't want to be openly embarrassed by the omission, so he continued to put it off.

"It just happened," she said. "Did you ever get stuck into something and then not know how to get out?"

Bill thought of an old girlfriend. He nodded.

"But I'm out now." She smiled and touched his hand. "Thanks to you."

Bill felt embarrassed, but he also felt pleased. He was beginning to feel less self-conscious. "But why me?" he asked.

"Because…," she paused and pressed her hands flat out on the table and stared at them, "because when I looked at your eyes in the bar, I just felt that you," she looked up at him, "could understand. Look, I know that you are…uh…young, but I just felt that I could trust you, and I haven't felt I could trust anyone for…." Her voice trailed off as she again looked down at the table, but then she looked back up and started again.

"Who are you anyway? I mean, I know you're probably a sailor but, well, do you know what I mean?"

Bill knew what she meant, and although he took no conscious notice of it, he looked at her and smiled. He had no formulated answer planned out in his brain, but he felt that he knew the answer, so he began.

"I'm a person who can see other people. By 'see,' I guess I mean sense how they feel." Bill picked up the saltshaker and focused his eyes on it causing the image of the girl to be blurred in the background. "Someday", he said, "someday, I might develop the ability to…uh…to handle this understanding, or…. uh…. sense of other people and use it to help me communicate." He put down the shaker and looked at the girl directly. Her eyes said more than words could and gave him the assurance to continue. "Now, it's not that way. Seeing people as I do only makes me and them uncomfortable."

"I don't feel that way," the girl said managing a slight smile.

"No, I know," Bill said. "It's because you're not pretending. He looked intently into her eyes, and he felt she understood. "And that's it. It's the pretending I can't handle. You see, it's like a mask that people wear or…," Bill smiled, "like a mirror— a mirror for others to see themselves in, to reflect their own gestures so they can react to them in ways that are as rehearsed and superficial as a commercial.

"I recall being at a party once when a girl who was making the rounds taking to everyone finally got to me. She asked a few questions to pick up some cues, and then she went from there to being what she considered 'charming.' She bounced one question after another off me, but from her eyes and mannerisms, I was sure she wasn't really interested. And, after one particular question—I can't even remember what it was—I asked her why she wanted to know. She didn't really have an answer for that, and after acting uncomfortable for a small while, she went away."

Bill looked at the girl's eyes, and she looked back. She didn't stare. She looked, and her eyes, for the moment, released the despair. He smiled, and she returned the same; and the seconds that traveled as hours at the tavern returned without their agony. The atmosphere at the pizza parlor no longer mattered, for Bill was sharing a real connection with someone who needed and accepted his offered openness, and this left no room for concern for "phony" places or saying the wrong thing.

Without the self-protective hurdles that Bill so often tripped over during initial socialization, he began to know comfort with the other person. The girl too, easily slipped into a casual and mutual insight. This singleness was bonded by personalities that chose, interpreted, and revealed with a double edge.

Eventually, the girl laughed as she threw back her head to flip her long hair over her shoulder. "I like you," she said. "I don't think you would hurt anyone."

"That's it," Bill said. "It's the hurt, isn't it? You don't know how to escape from it."

The girl stiffened. "I won't go back to him," she said. "I'm through with that."

"That's not what I meant," Bill said. "Your hurt doesn't come from someone else—not the hurt I feel that you have. You can leave him behind, but unless you leave behind what's inside you tearing you down, you'll be no better off."

The girl put her arms on the table and turned them over, so her palms were facing up. "I once tried to commit suicide," she said looking down at her wrists.

Bill looked at the scars on her wrists. "You can move on from it without destroying yourself," he said putting his hands over hers.

The girl smiled a weak smile and some of the spark came back into her eyes. "Will you help me?" she asked.

"As much as I can," Bill said and then laughed a nervous laugh, feeling a slight uneasiness. "Sometimes, I don't feel qualified enough to help myself."

"I like you," the girl said, this time in a softer and more serious tone. "I can talk to you," she squeezed his hands, "and you're not mean."

"I guess I find it easy to talk to you too," Bill said. "It's not like that with most people. Often, I just can't say the right thing. I try hard, because I'm concerned about fitting in. I usually end up embarrassing myself, though. I realize that I'm very insecure. I've even spent a lot of time contemplating the deep psychological reasons behind it. Sometimes, I think that by just admitting to myself how I feel somehow makes up for not being as much as I'd like to be."

"At least you're honest."

"I'd rather be rich," Bill said, repeating a cliché stored and readily and automatically retrieved from memory. "By the way, my name's Bill."

The girl smiled again, a fuller, more open smile than before. "Mine's Janice."

"Are you really an epileptic?"

"Yes. Does that bother you?"

Bill shrugged. "No." He was going to ask her if she had noticed his eye condition, but he decided not to. "What about your pills?" he asked. "Do you need them? Do you have any more?"

"I have one more bottle back at the apartment. "Will you—" the girl stopped and glanced down, and then she looked back up again, "will you help me move out?" she said quickly.

"Is the guy that was in the bar your husband?"

"No—but I was—well, he lives in the same apartment, but we weren't—"

Bill held his hand up. "It doesn't matter," he said. "You sure that's what you want?"

"I have to." She shook her head. "I can't, anymore, no more." She looked up at him. "I shouldn't involve you. He's mean, you know. And sometimes he gets wild and does crazy things."

"I know," Bill said more to himself than to the girl.

"He's probably back there waiting for me right now. Maybe we'd better not. I don't know...."

Bill looked at his watch. "I think we have some time." He got up and took her hand. "We'd better get moving though. C'mon."

V

Bill carried the girl's suitcase into the lobby of the southern hotel. He had asked the cab driver to take them to a cheap but clean hotel and this was where they ended up. It had seemed a suitable place when the cab pulled up in front, but the fare had come to more than he expected.

He set the bags down in front of the desk and looked up at the thin gray-haired man who had watched them enter the hotel. "How much are your single rooms?" Bill asked.

The man answered looking from Bill to the girl.

"You have a weekly rate?" Bill asked.

The man looked at him and then the girl. "Yes, but—uh, you have to establish yourself as a preferred tenant first."

Bill picked up the chained pen in front of the register book and started writing—"Miss Janice—" he looked up at the girl.

"Johnson," the girl said.

The man stood staring at him with his tight-pressed lips showing a slight tinge of blue.

Bill handed the man some cash. "For five days," he said.

The man handed him change and placed a key on the counter. He looked at the girl. "You can use the elevator over there," he said. "Room 213."

"Thanks." Bill slipped the key into his shirt pocket. "I'm just going to help her take her bags up—I don't plan on staying." Right after he said that, he wished that he hadn't; he didn't figure it should have been necessary to explain his intentions.

The hotel clerk was still staring after them as they disappeared into the elevator.

VI

One of the suitcases lay spread open on the bed, but no clothes had been removed. The girl was lying on her back with her head propped on the pillow and one leg dangling over the edge of the bed. "I'm exhausted," she said.

Bill, who had been facing away from her, staring out the window down at the street, turned and looked at her. "I'm going to get out of here, so you can get some rest."

The girl sat up quickly. "No, don't go. I didn't mean it like that."

Bill laughed. "I know. It's just that I think—well, you've had a rough day and I know you're tired—and besides I have a headache, I could use some rest too. Oh Christ! See what I mean? Look, I'm sorry—I sound like an idiot. It's just that I feel that you need to do some thinking. You have to decide what you want before you get involved in anything else—and that includes me."

She was standing up waiting for him, as he walked toward the door. "Thanks," she said as she kissed him lightly. He heard her voice, but it was her eyes that carried the message the loudest.

"Think about going home," he said, or at least later he thought he remembered having said it. "Think about going home—I'll still put you on the bus, you know."

"I know. You are sweet. Will I see you again?"

"I have duty tomorrow. I'll be off Monday afternoon, though. About four. Will you be here?"

"I'll be here," she said and maybe she said something else, but Bill couldn't remember. He was walking down the hall feeling good.

When he stepped out of the elevator, he was still smiling. The hotel clerk seemed surprised to see him just ten minutes after he had gone up. "Just a quickie," Bill said as he walked past the desk, still with the same foolish grin on his face.

Once back out in the bright late afternoon sunshine, his grin disappeared. He stared up at the second floor of the hotel trying to pick out the right window, but he couldn't. He started walking down the street, and he considered going into one of the Go-Go bars along the way, but his headache really was coming back, and he wasn't up to having another drink.

Ahead, walking in the same direction, was a young man, obviously a sailor, Bill thought, walking on wobbly legs with his arm draped over the shoulders of a fat, dark-haired girl. Their togetherness seemed to provide more mutual support than affection. An older lady walking by in the opposite direction glanced at the couple and then quickly looked away. She looked at Bill. *I'm not one of them,* Bill's thoughts called out, but his voice was silent as the lady passed him by.

He no longer felt good. He wondered what he would do and after considering going to a movie, he finally decided that he couldn't afford it if he was going to have enough money left to last him until payday. He finally decided to go back to the boat.

As he stood at the bus stop waiting for the Ballast Point bus, he felt as alone and miserable as he had earlier. He thought of Janice and this produced a temporary satisfaction and even anticipation for the coming of Monday, but in the back of his mind, a familiar voice—that reminded him of Parsons—kept nagging at him. "You're a fool," the voice accused.

Chapter VI

Most of me accepts the joke
And laughter is the pay
Most of me believes that it
Is really the best way
And it's most of me
That will keep on going
And not listen very long
To the part of me that
Believes there's more
And wonders what went wrong

—Bill

Sunday passed slowly for Bill without incident. He stood two four-hour SMAW (shutdown maneuvering area watch) training watches back in maneuvering, did some weekly P.M. (preventive maintenance) on the portable tools, and he even managed to watch a movie without being challenged for being a non-qual. Several times, he had tried to call Janice at the hotel, but she hadn't been in her room.

At the Monday morning breakfast, he was surprised to find that more than half the crew had showed up. He thought this unusual because at sea, breakfast was the only meal that didn't have two calls and even then, the mess was never more than half full. Today, however, the mess tables were all jammed tight and there were people in the passageway waiting their turn for a seat. Bill had sat down early so he found a seat. One of the qualified men who had been left standing up had challenged him for his seat, but Bill decided that it was a half-hearted gesture, so he remained seated and said nothing and the man didn't feel compelled to back up his effort.

Bill would learn later that a Monday morning breakfast in port was always crowded—mostly because the single Johns, who had not taken much time out for "chowing down" on the beach, would come back to the ship hungry—hung over maybe, but still hungry.

He hadn't seen Parsons since the ship pulled in, but he knew he was in the mess because, occasionally, he could hear his characteristic cackle. The whole mess was noisy, however, because all the men who didn't feel too sick or sorry were relating the stories of their weekend entertainment.

"...glad when we leave for West-Pac," someone was saying. "My bod just can't tolerate much more of this sweet punishment. Hey, Doc, is it possible to thrash yourself to death?"

"No, but if you dunk your dipstick into a rotten snapper, it might fall off," the corpsman answered.

"Aw, Doc, you take the fun out of everything."

"You uncouth son-of-bitch!" someone hollered.

Bill looked above several heads to the center of the room and saw Gabby waving someone's arm in the air.

"Look, you guys, he's got shit under his fingernails." He dropped the hand. "Yuck! How can you come to the table like that?"

"Christ," the sailor said, seemingly unembarrassed, "haven't you ever heard of a finger wave? Really turns them on. You ought to try it."

"You ought to try washing your hands."

"What for? Sleeping, eating, and sticking my finger up a girl's ass—that's my joy in life. And if the three of them get a little mixed in together, well, that's all right too."

"You're missing out on the finest joy of all," another voice contributed. "You haven't lived till you've had your O-ring marinated with spit from a slithery tongue."

"How about one of Snorkel Patty's hot water hummers?" someone else added.

Bill tried to imagine sticking his finger up Janice's ass, but the thought repulsed him, and he felt guilty for considering it. He thought about making love to her, but even this left him uncomfortable. It wasn't that he didn't feel the desire to make love to her, or that he was a novice at such things, it was just that it didn't seem right. He reasoned that she probably would let him, perhaps she even expected him to do it, but even that didn't make it right in his own mind.

He knew that she had been to bed with other men—probably many other men; even he could tell that. But he was different—he had to be different. He couldn't take a little bit more of her, because he understood that there was little left. If he screwed—fucked her (he winched as he made himself think in those terms)—well, he just couldn't do that without making an implied promise. Oh, there had been other girls and there had been no promises with them. But they were different—they were screwing him too. But girls like Janice were another matter—you couldn't screw girls like Janice without making an implied promise. Unless, of course, you were a real bastard—and Bill didn't like to consider himself as a real bastard.

The mess room conversation broke into Bill's thoughts.

"Jesus, you're a regular pre-vert, you know that?"

The sailor shrugged. "Isn't everybody?"

Chapter VII

Someone said, "I'll be your friend"
I didn't ask him why
Someone said, "Come follow along"
I just said I'd try
Another person said, "How come?
Why are you so meek?"
I turned to him to assert myself
But I had no voice to speak

—Anonymous

I

When Bill got off that afternoon, he hurried to the locker club, changed his clothes, and then boarded a bus for downtown San Diego. Parsons had asked him earlier if he wanted to go out to the Red Garter drinking, but he had refused saying that he had an appointment to see a girl. This was not exactly the truth—he had attempted to reach Janice several times by phone during the day, but he hadn't found her in.

It took a half hour for the bus to reach Bill's destination, and this ride, in a way, seemed like an endless one. But, in another respect, as if measured by a separate consciousness, it was over all too quickly. During the ride, he kept seeking self-assurance that he really should see Janice again. But this notwithstanding, his path was set, and he knew that, although perhaps he could, he wouldn't turn back. He briefly wondered at the worth of seeking a relationship that he knew could not last very long, but he pushed these thoughts aside. He reasoned that no relationship is permanent and that the very fact that one can be developed is justification enough for doing so.

He had never turned his back on an offered friendship. On many occasions, he even allowed himself to be deliberately used by people whose intent was buried beneath a guise of friendship. He was never really fooled, though; he just seemed to lack, what, in moments of reflection, he called the inner strength to throw off these demands made by people who, he felt, secretly laughed at him.

When acknowledging deliberate thoughts, Bill reasoned that by continuing evenly and resolutely along his way, the people who occasionally hitched a ride would only serve to strengthen his ability and allow easier movement for much of the way. Inner impulses, however, often urged him to shake off the unwanted burdens as a wolf might shake off drops of water, and such an image, although appealing, only had clarity when separated from the causes that created it.

Bill wondered at his growing friendship with Parsons. He reasoned that if Parsons was using him, that he was using Parsons as well. He didn't regret the relationship, and he was beginning to understand what, at first, he would have denied. He acknowledged to himself that he and Parsons had much in common.

By searching within himself, he could find the same cynical skepticism that bubbled on the surface of Parsons. It wasn't easily exposed, but Parsons wasn't gentle about tearing it out. And this, Bill believed, was why Parsons originally sought him out and would continue to do so. He too enlisted a certain buried characteristic from deep within Parsons. And he too, in his own way, was no gentler in pulling to the surface that hidden aspect which in him was very easily exposed. Yes, he recognized his sensitivity. He was proud of it. He worked at it and considered it a strength, not a weakness.

Bill didn't really expect to find Janice at the hotel when he arrived. Of course, this was just a feeling, and he hadn't translated it into thought, but as he faced the hotel clerk across the counter, he experienced consciously what had been knowable all along. He was not surprised when the clerk handed him the letter. He even understood what was inside. Not the words, the words would be only imperfect reductions; the letter would contain the rationalization of what Janice had already expressed directly without words.

Bill knew. And, in knowing, he also knew why part of him had been reluctant to come. He could have come close to answering Janice's needs—close, but missing only in that by trying, he would be compromising his own needs. For he realized that he could provide Janice with the comfort she needed only if he could remain satisfied in doing so. And he knew that this satisfaction would not remain strong enough to keep him from searching somewhere else, in someone else, for the strength that she didn't have.

But even if that inward voice had been stronger, he would still have come. For as futile as the trip had been, or as inadequate the initial aspiration was, Bill was easily swayed by the wants and needs of others, even if responding to such needs meant disregarding, for the time being, that vague and undefined goal toward which his inner consciousness kept drawing him back.

II

The cab had already gone several miles before he opened the letter. He read it over several times. The part about being the nicest person she had ever met he read only once, but the rest, the parts about her marrying and moving away, he read over and over. In a way, it seemed strange that she didn't mention anything about who she was going to marry. It could be just some sailor that she had just met, but it wasn't. He knew who she was marrying, and he also knew that it was not very likely that she was moving away.

Her letter pretended that she was happy, but he understood that this was for his benefit—this was so he didn't have to understand where she was or why. And, although he did understand and felt sorry, he couldn't feel regret. But still, it bothered him.

He closed his eyes and imagined things that troubled him, but he didn't try to shut these things out. He had visions of Janice standing in a room that looked like a kitchen surrounded by five children. The children, fighting, crying, clinging, and clawing, looked like they were made of ginger bread and each one appeared to have some missing part, almost as if it had been bitten off. And her face, devoid of individual personality, was not just her face—it was the face of all the people, who having withdrawn from expectation, are left with only the day-to-day transient expressions—dulled suffering and listless smiles without joy or hope.

"Here you are," the cab driver said as he turned around and looked at Bill.

Bill looked out the window and stared at the large plastic red garter that rotated on the roof of the cocktail lounge. He stared at the bright red door and wondered if Parsons was still there, and he wondered what he would do if he wasn't.

Chapter VIII

Going to sea is great for me
The only way I have
To make the money that I need
And some to spare
But believe me when I say
I'd rather throw my coin away
Than to stay out there and be a millionaire

—Radio Station S.T.U.D.

I

Bill stood behind the throttle man in maneuvering. He wore a headset with one ear covered by the cushioned earpiece positioned toward the back of his head leaving one ear open to the maneuvering room conversation. The headset was plugged into the JA phone circuit that linked together the phone talkers in control, the bridge, and DC forward and aft. Also, various stations on the sub had communications links via the 7MC, the 21MC, and (in the case of the engineering spaces) the 2MC and the X60J phone circuit.

The engineering officer of the watch gave directions and received requests and replies from the engineering watch stations on the X60J sound-powered phone circuit that had an amplifying speaker in maneuvering. During the maneuvering watch, many phone stations were manned with most of the information being relayed, interpreted, and passed on through the phone talkers on the sound-powered phone circuits. The MCs, which announced their messages to many at the same time, were used judiciously as most of the relayed information had a focused destination that could be acknowledged quickly by phone to phone tie-ups.

Bill, with his ears tuned to the phone messages, the MCs maneuvering amplifier, the maneuvering room conversations, and the background noises, experienced a unique auditory initiation at the beginning of the journey of mind and time in the still new portable world.

"Cast off number four line."

"…long time to be gone. I wonder if the wife will be…."

"Cast off number four, aye."

"Don't worry, she'll find some jarhead to keep her primed."

"Maneuvering, Bridge, back one-third."

"Bridge, Maneuvering, back one-third, aye."

Bill felt the sensation of motion as the screw sliced through the water and propelled the sub away from the pier.

"Carbary, you keep the bell log."

"Back two-thirds."

"Back two-thirds, Maneuvering, aye."

"A.E.A. to Maneuvering."

"Answering back two-thirds."

"I always have duty the day before we leave on one of these extended cruises. It just doesn't seem…"

"Patterson's busy. Whaddaya need?"

"They got those cables down from the trunk yet?"

"They're just getting them down."

"Ahead one-third, aye."

"It'll take more than three weeks before we hit Naha."

"It's a lot better than that T.J. stuff, I'll tell you that."

"Maneuvering, Tunnel, permission to secure the sight glass watch?"

"Answering ahead one-third."

"He still up there?"

"Course, it's all a matter of taste. I understand Carbary's pretty hot for that Mexican food."

"Maneuvering, Bridge, rig the engineering spaces for dive."

"They want us to rig for dive."

"Very well. A.E.A. come to Maneuvering. Goddamnit! Aren't those cables down yet?"

"He's in one of those moods."

"His wife probably didn't give him any last night. Hey, Mr. Browder, where's a good place to go in Naha?"

"Watch your panel."

"Ahead two-thirds."

"Ahead two-thirds, aye."

"Where are we going, anyway? I mean after Naha."

"Answering ahead two-thirds."

"Who gives a shit? It's all the same. We might as well submerge next to the pier."

"Maneuvering, Tunnel, permission to secure the sight-glass watch?"

"Is he still up there?"

"Tell him to secure."

"Secure."

"Hayes, use proper phone procedure."

"Aw, Mr. Browder, don't get chicken shit. We're at sea now."

"All stations, Maneuvering, rig the engineering spaces for dive."

"I'm sick of this, let's go home."

"I'm just sick. I want to hit the rack. When are they going to secure the maneuvering watch?"

"We just started. We'll be here for an hour yet at least. What section's got the first watch?"

"Section two."

"Section two always has it first."

"You're not in section two anymore. Didn't you check the new watch, Bill?"

"Oh, hell. How can you keep track of what they do anyway? Why'd they go fucking with the sections? I suppose they stuck me with those nerds in section three."

"Hayes, watch your panel."

II

Any one day was very much like the one that came before and the one that would come next. In fact, time didn't seem to be divided in twenty-four-hour periods but rather by the eight-hour intervals that separated each four-hour watch. Daytime soon became practically indistinguishable from night time, with the only indicator being the twenty-four-hour clock in the torpedo room, the rig for red condition of the control room during darkness (so eye adjustment would not hinder night periscope vision), and the fact that the noon meal was a formal one and the midnight one was not.

Bill spent about three hours of each off-watch period sleeping. It bothered him at first to adjust to this but soon he managed as everyone else did and after the first four days, he was even able to shit regularly. He spent an additional three hours of off-watch time qualifying. He studied books, crawled behind panels and underneath pipes, traced electrical circuits and sea-water pipes, interpreted color codes, and analyzed nuclear theories. And, as he examined each piece and system, he tried to consider it as it related to the whole submarine, which itself was a unit of many contributing parts.

Considered only as a whole, the submarine was as overwhelming as a scrambled jigsaw puzzle, but part by part, with the whole in mind, the pattern became discernible. The submarine carried Bill through the deep, cold, dark sea. It protected him with its thick iron shell, gave him light to see, water to drink, and carried the food that he ate.

The huge steam pipes that carried power to the shaft, heated his working spaces, and so that this heat didn't become overbearing, the dual air-conditioning plants, aided by the multi-speed electric blowers, sent dehumidified air to cool him. The submarine was his protector and provider. He was aware that the world of the submarine was not a completely isolated one. There were outputs from and to this world that simplified its existence as not even temporarily self-purposeful, but the illusion was there. The submarine needed to be known and Bill needed to know and this much at this time was enough.

The remaining two hours he had left between watches, he spent eating, talking, watching a movie, or just doing nothing. Doing nothing wasn't as easy on a submarine as it was in many other places. And, to meet all of what he considered to be the requirements, Bill had to work at it.

If there were any others on the sub who occasionally engaged in doing nothing, they probably did it in their rack. Bill never asked anyone—he just supposed this to be the case. But it was not an adequate place for him. He had to be somewhere where no one would think to look for him. To be free from other's knowledge was an absolute requirement— otherwise his mind would not be released from worrying that someone might bother him.

He found his place outboard of the RPPW (reactor plant fresh water) pumps in the lower level AMS. There was an area there that he could wiggle into and remain almost completely hidden with a small chance of being detected by an occasional roving watch stander. The space was uncomfortable, but this was not important. For ten or fifteen minutes, he could forget the discomfort of the bend of a pipe pressing against his back and just let his mind wander. Even though his mind worked, it was not consciously directed by a purpose, and during these occasional moments of solitude, he was complete within himself. Ever since he could remember, he had sought out such moments to himself. Although he didn't understand how or why, he knew that it helped him and gave him a direction.

He was assigned as a trainee on the eight-to-twelve AEA (auxiliary electrician aft) watch. On the sub, there were two auxiliary electrical watch standers at any one time—one roved the forward spaces and one roved the after-engineering spaces. The formal duties of the AEA were to hourly monitor and record the readings on the temperature monitoring panels (TMs), periodically rove the engineering spaces observing and manually feeling motors for signs of malfunction or overheating, and to be on hand in case of fire or flooding to manually secure any power source or electrical equipment that might be a cause or contributor to the emergency.

One of the first and most important of the formal duties drilled into all novice roving watch standers was, as a first course of action, to immediately secure any compartment in which existed any hint of impending danger. This would mean, of course, that it was a good possibility that it would be an AEA who would remain in the isolated compartment to take further action against the danger. But, when considering that a high-pressure steam leak would roast the entire crew instantaneously, a one-inch unchecked sea-water leak at 300 feet would barely allow enough time to close the watertight doors and secure ventilation. And, an un-isolated fire could send suffocating smoke swiftly throughout a submerged submarine. It didn't really matter who went first. It was generally understood, however, that AEAs were expendable.

Such were the formal duties of the AEA. And such formal duties were the responsibility of the formal watch stander. An occasional additional formal duty of the AEA (or any other watch stander) was to give instructions to trainees. This duty was not actually a burden, however, for although the formal watch stander had to take time to give instruction, he was allowed to unload the informal duties of his watch station on the trainee.

The informal duty of the AEA was to act as a runner for the immobile watch standers. Also, since the AEA was an initiatory watch, it was only natural that one of the unspoken informal duties of the AEA would be to act as a fall-guy for any kind of practical joke or prank that any of the more qualified "sitter" watch standers thought up to pass the time.

Of course, there were the old stand-by routines that had been pulled since ships were powered by sails, but still the supply of naïve new guys never ran short and all the 'been-arounders" knew where next to send the frustrated trainee who was tracking down a "main bearing." Then there were those pranks that were too obvious for the direct approach and required a lead-up. It would be a very naïve new guy who would be foolish enough to stick a funnel in his waistband when someone was standing around holding a cup of cold water, but when a bunch of guys are having a contest to see who can drop a washer off his nose into the funnel the most number of times, then the "fish" is usually more than eager to join in. This approach is so effective that it has been known to work more than once on the same man. This classic prank uses such a lead-up, and Bill was fortunate enough to see it pulled on someone else before he himself was fished into it.

Patterson, the EWS (engineering watch stander), stuck his head into maneuvering and said to Bill, "After you take those readings, c'mon into the AMS. We'll go through the rig for dive check-off again."

"Sure," Bill said, "be right in."

When he entered the AMS, he noticed many men gathered around the electrician's bench apparently having some sort of contest using the vise which was fastened to the bench.

"Where's Patterson?" Bill asked as he watched one of the men tightening down the clamps of the vise on another man's thumbs.

"Ah…Ah…Ah…that's it!" the man cried.

Someone pulled out a tape and measured the distance from the edge of the bench to the end of the handle. The handle was released, a chart was taken off the wall, and someone wrote on it. "Ten and a half! That's a new record," he said.

"Where's Patterson?" Bill repeated as he inched closer to look at the chart that contained a long list of names and endurance distances.

"He's busy," someone said. "Said for you to wait."

"I can better that last mark," Hayes said as he came forward wiggling both thumbs in the air.

Bill watched intently as the vise was clamped down on his thumbs. Someone held the tape in place as the handle was inched toward the previous mark—9 ½—10—10 ½—

"…uh…uh…uh…give me another half inch," Hayes grunted.

"What a whore," someone said.

"What are they doing?" someone asked pushing himself up alongside of Bill.

"Huh?" Bill turned to look at one of the new mess cooks who had just delivered a pot of coffee to the maneuvering watch standers. "Oh, it's some kind of endurance contest."

"Eleven inches! Jesus, if you were ever captured, they'd never make you talk."

"If they put his nuts in there, they would."

"Let me try it," the mess cook said pushing to the front.

The man on the handle shrugged and made room for the mess cook to position his thumbs in the clamp. When the vice was tightened down, Hayes reached over and unfastened the man's belt.

"Hey, what are you doing?"

"Go get the grease gun," Hayes said, as he pushed the man's pants and shorts down to his ankles.

Bill found the vise prank extremely funny, but he wasn't sure how he would have taken it had his end been on the receiving end. He was on the receiving end of the errand boy status, however, and he soon came to learn that the announced command "AEA, come to maneuvering" generally meant that someone had a trivial mission to send him on. The maneuvering watches usually referred informally to the "AEA" as the 'gopher' (go-for), but Parsons had a more colorful title for the position which Bill was aspiring to—he just called him the "After Nigger." He was making a comparison with the forward stewards, who were not black at all but Guamanians, but Parsons seldom let, what he would term as, 'minor distinctions' interfere with his view of life.

Even with the roving, the monitoring, and the errand running, Bill found that he still had considerable free time while standing the AEA watch. At first, he would use this time studying an RPM or tracing out an electrical or seawater system, but soon he began to use part of his watch time just for shooting the shit with the other watch standers in the section. They still ran him on errands and went through the motions of giving him a hard time, but it was more of a ritual than a test, and he accepted it knowing that it was part of his acceptance, and he gave back the same.

Sometimes he felt guilty about using his time so loosely, but gradually, he became consciously aware that it was necessary in a very serious way. He made the rounds and listened to the sea stories and, as the weeks went by, he soon started to pick up the re-runs. He realized that the stories themselves didn't really matter and that most of the in-section watch standers had shared their experiences many times, but they never seemed to tire of doing it again.

Thus, Bill took his first steps towards becoming something other than a non-qual. And it wasn't in his growing knowledge of the submarine alone, or even to the greatest degree, which gave him his accepted status; it was the qualification of and the compensation for this knowledge that made the difference and made his education more than one-sided.

This compensation was, in a way, paradoxical—for it was pretending to love, by exaggeration and understatement, what was unpleasant, and in a similar sense, holding seemingly high regard for the truly unpleasant. So, it was with being at sea—almost never did the submarine enlisted man openly analyze a sea voyage as being anything but an almost unbearable burden or as a romantic adventure. These views, although perhaps not realistic, were purposeful—for they provided a group cohesiveness and camaraderie that made time pass more quickly and colored both the moment and the memory.

Chapter IX

We pulled into Naha
We collected our pay
We thought that we'd
Be there for many a day
But one night of duty
And one liberty
And the raunchy ol' Sculpin
She'd pulled out to sea

—Radio Station S.T.U.D.

There are inner things I think about
There are feelings I don't express
There are events that I'm ashamed of
Only inwardly do I confess
These things that I keep inside
They show in little ways
And the people who can read these signs
Often catch my gaze
But a person that I know
Can see, and look and not pretend
To be better in his knowing; this
Person is my friend

—Bill

I

Naha, Okinawa. Picturesque. Quaint shops. Narrow streets. Japanese girls. Kimonos. American dresses. Japanese-American girls. Soldiers and sailors. Military police and shore patrol. Country and western music. Beer. American money.

Sidewalk shops. Merchants. Girl back home. Mother. Gift. Price bargaining. American money.

Uniforms. Dusty streets. Cheap shops. Peddlers. Clip joints. Shit-kicking music. Booze. Hootch. American money.

G.I.s. M.P.s. Shitheads. Dirt. Street-walkers. Pimps. Mama-San. Papa-San. What the hell does "San" mean? Junk shops. Haggling. American money.

Whores. Hotels. American loneliness. American lust. American money. American must.

II

When Bill stepped out onto the pier in Naha, Okinawa, the world seemed somehow different. Things, like a blue sky and a fresh breeze, once taken for granted, now seemed an unusual and valuable experience. The crisp Okinawa December day permeated his senses and somewhat reminded him of winter days in Ohio. He thought back to Decembers in his hometown, but remembered events and places seemed to blend into a union of sameness and thus separate his present experience and make it seem far removed by time and perception.

He understood that time's progression was continuous, but he himself, his consciousness and personality as the reference point, perceived time's movements, often staying static, advancing very quickly, or moving immediately from one point to the next with no connection with the in-between. He could be closer or farther from the past than just the distance of the yesterdays. Sometimes, the seemingly never changing similarity of everyday experience would briefly seem different and surreal. This was usually just a feeling, sometimes sharp and painfully repelling, and sometimes just a brief longing dulled by loneliness, doubt, and denial. It was never long or clear enough to be fully incorporated and understood in his time related physical 'now.'

III

It was cold and crisp. The brisk weather was hardly noticeable. The group of sailors, with a bantering spirit, enclosed in heavy woolen uniforms, walked with a light-hearted cadence toward a new and long-anticipated experience.

After several beers, the large original groups had split into many smaller ones, each progressing through similar experiences, only some more frantic than others. Naha seemed like a rat's maze; however, no one experienced an inaccessible door, nor was consciously frustrated, or fully aware, that no door provided an entrance to quite the level of experience that had been imagined.

Bill, Gabby, and Parsons walked together down one of the narrow streets. Somewhere between where they had started and where they would finish was a confrontation with what they expected. This was neither a burden nor a quest, but it was an identifier like and not totally apart from the uniform that wrapped and protected but also influenced the men within.

"Button up that P-coat, Sailor." The shore patrol stuck his head back in the window, and the van continued slowly down the street.

"Fuck them," Bill said putting his hands in the pockets of the still opened coat.

"You better do it," Parsons said," that shithead is sure to be back."

"So, we'll kick some ass," Gabby said. "Let them come back."

"Yeah, we could probably do that. I'd enjoy it too. But later," Parsons said. "No sense in being hauled back to the boat without experiencing the full spectrum of pleasures.

Bill buttoned up his coat. *What the hell,* he thought; he was cold anyway.

IV

Laughter, that's what makes it different, Bill thought as he looked around the bar where he was currently parked. Different from what? He shook his head quickly. Oh, not from the other bars in Naha. They all had laughter. But maybe it wasn't the laughter. Or maybe this bar had better laughter? Bill smiled. That must be it all right; the other bars had inferior laughter. How many beers had he had? Shit, who cares? He guessed that beer gave him insight. He wondered if his insight was cross-eyed, because his outsight was cross-eyed. He laughed out loud—Parsons would love that.

"Hey, Frank," Bill said thumping him on the shoulder. Parsons spun around on his bar stool almost spilling the girl who was sitting on his lap. "Hey, where's yours?" he asked.

Bill looked around at the base of his bar stool. "I think she went to pee," he said with a grin. What happened to Gabby?

"He couldn't wait," Parsons said. "He fell in love."

"Here's to love," Bill said, while trying to take a drink and at the same time remember what it was that he had been thinking about. I'll never give in, he thought at last without really realizing why it occurred to him.

"You buy me drink?"

Bill looked at the girl and tried to decide if it was the same one that he had been buying drinks for before. He guessed that it was and tried to remember her name.

He had taken a memory course once that taught him to associate some familiar object, having a name like that of the person's name he desired to remember, to a particular characteristic of that person's face or appearance. He studied the girl's face and, for some reason, envisioned first a beard and then an electric shaver—the kind with the three rotary heads. He looked at the girl through his half empty beer glass. "Norelco!" he cried.

"Noreco," the girl corrected. "You buy me drink, Bill-San?"

Bill's memory was picking up speed now, and he started to re-appreciate the assets that he had so carefully noted when he had approached the girl earlier—or had she approached him? Her shiny black hair, piled up intricately on top of her head, came about level to Bill's chin. Her facial features were soft with dark eyes, a nose that was short with only a hint of broadness, and a small mouth colored with a glistening red lipstick. She was wearing a shiny satin-like dress that clung to her slim figure. Unlike the other girls, she had a pair of tits that were round and firm and stuck out enough so that Bill had the inclination to cup them with his hands to help hold them up in case they might droop under their own weight.

He thought about the fantasy that one of the sailors had related while at sea. This sailor had said that his most fervent desire upon getting back to civilization was to run barefoot through a field of naked women lying in the sun with their breasts pointed toward the blue sky. Bill smiled; he had said "civilization." He figured that, perhaps, civilization was a place where there were more civilians than military types. In that case, a field full of naked women would certainly qualify. He reached out and brushed one of the girl's breasts with the back of his hand.

"He'd probably trip over this," he said out loud. Bill had always fancied himself as a leg man, but as he anticipated and envisioned, his center of focus was bordered by her long black hair, loosened and hanging down to her round little ass and cascading over the sides of her body while two melon sized breasts swung back and forth and lightly brushed his own chest, as she teased and enticed him suggesting an experience that he expected would surpass his imagination.

She reached out and glided her hand smoothly up and down Bill's arm. "You like Noreco?" she asked.

Bill got goose bumps all over, and, although he had intentions of being cool, the most composed thing he could think to do was to stick a pretzel in his mouth and nod.

"You pay Mama-San," the girl said. It was not a question, it was an answer—Bill's eyes had asked the question.

Bill reached for his wallet and asked how much.

Noreco put her hands behind Bill's neck and pulled his face to her while she stretched up on her toes to meet him. Her kiss was soft and warm and the brief and darting touch of her tongue seemed to cause the strength and the remnants of composure to drain from the upper parts of his body and concentrate in what he knows must be a record-breaking hard-on, which pushed against the restraining thirteen-button flap like a trap waiting to spring.

"You pay Mama-San now," Noreco said, as she dropped her hands from his neck and casually brushed his flap-covered bulge, "I will be back soon." She walked toward the curtain-covered doorway around to the side and behind the bar.

When she disappeared from sight, Bill refocused his sight on the small gray-haired woman who was standing directly in front of him behind the bar. At first, Bill thought she wanted to know if he wanted another drink, but then his mind slipped back into gear and he understood. Bill pulled out his wallet and put a ten on the bar.

Mama-San continued to stare at him. He continued to place bills on the bar until she smiled and picked them up.

Bill guessed that the procedure was somewhat like that of the sidewalk merchants, but he couldn't bring himself to bicker about the cost of a prize that he wanted at any price. As he watched the money disappear, he realized that he would have been disappointed if the cost had come cheaply.

Just as appropriately as she had left, Noreco reappeared wearing a heavy red woolen coat. She slipped her arm through

Bill's and looked up at him smiling. "Noreco like Bill-San," she said.

Bill turned back toward the bar to get his hat, but just as he did, it came flying up toward his face. He jumped back and grabbed it. "What'd ya do that for?" he asked, looking at Parsons.

"I just wanted to see if you had enough extra skin left over to blink," Parsons said grinning.

"We're leaving," Bill said nodding towards Noreco. "I guess we're going to a hotel."

"You're going to get fucked," Parsons said with the same grin on his face. He had a look in his eyes, however, that caused Bill, for a moment to wonder at what he meant.

"Why don't you pay Mama-San and come along with yours?" Bill asked, hoping that he wouldn't and then hoping that Parsons wouldn't understand that hope and the reason behind it.

"You go ahead," Parsons said. "I'm not done getting drunk yet."

V

The old Naha Petty Officers' Club was built to be a service related benefit for sailors and other uniformed personal and money had been liberally spent when it was planned. It resembled a classy state-side restaurant, but the prices were cheap and the atmosphere was open to the mood of the clientele. When Bill and Noreco entered, there were few people there, and he had selected an out of the way table in a corner.

Just like a regular date, Bill thought as he lifted the piece of steak to his mouth and looked across at Noreco. She eats just like anyone else, his thoughts continued. Doesn't talk much, though. He smiled. Of course, talking wasn't the important part. He was proud of himself that he was able to focus his thoughts on the heart of the matter—he knew that he was really becoming a qualified submariner. He realized that taking the girl to dinner had been a small weakness. He decided that he wouldn't mention this part of his experience on the boat.

"…on your submarine, Bill-San?"

"Huh?" Bill looked at Noreco. "Uh…excuse me…uh… I didn't hear what you said."

"Are you leaving soon on your submarine, Bill-San?"

Had he mentioned the submarine? He couldn't remember. Did she know that the name seen on his right shoulder was the name of a submarine? "Uh…no, we'll be here a while," he lied.

"Noreco like Bill-San." She reached over and put her hand on his. "Once before, Noreco had sailor boyfriend. He left on ship and then he never come back. Noreco think something happen to him. Bill-San tell Noreco where you go on your submarine so Noreco can pray that you come back and be safe."

Bill thought about asking her why she had to know where he was going so that she could pray for him, but he decided it was best just to sidetrack the whole conversation. He put his napkin down on the table and picked up the check. He reached across for Noreco's hand as he stood up. "I can't tell you, because I don't know. C'mon, let's go."

Noreco pulled her hand away and put both hands on her lap with her eyes down. "Bill-San don't like Noreco."

Bill sat back down and put his hand to his head. This isn't supposed to happen when you buy one he thought. Maybe the dinner had been a mistake. Maybe it was the girl. Had he gotten a bad one? Could he take her back and trade her? he joked to himself. Parsons had warned him, hadn't he? What had he said? Something, anyway. He really wanted her then, though. Now that he was a little soberer, he realized that she wasn't the dream girl he had thought she was.

She is probably even wearing falsies, he thought with a smile. He didn't even want her that much anymore. He had thought that eating dinner would settle his stomach, but he was beginning to feel a little sick. By God, he'd have her though. He'd paid for her. What was this shit she was pulling anyway? Why couldn't she stay quiet like he thought she would. What was with these questions? They had warned us about answering questions. She was probably some Commie. Christ, I wonder if she's clean? He looked at her again. Her mascara was running where the tears had rolled down her face.

"Noreco, don't cry," Bill said standing up again. He reached for her arm. "Look, I will tell you, okay? Don't cry."

She looked up at him. "You tell me now?"

"Uh, no, not now. Later, after we get to know each other better." Bill felt proud at this approach, but he fully expected the girl to burst into tears again.

Noreco stood up, but she did not look up at Bill. "Excuse please, Bill-San wait here," she said as she took her purse and started off in the direction of the ladies' room.

As Bill sat back down, he caught the attention of the waitress. He ordered another drink, and, as he sat waiting, he drummed his fingers up and down on the table, while he contemplated how unpredictably alike all women were. He figured if he kept his cool he could handle Noreco, but then he thought of Barbara, and he wasn't so sure.

The waitress sat his drink on the table and walked away. He didn't reach for it, however. He just stared transfixed on another time and place, as his mind drifted.

* * *

Why am I doing this? Bill thought as he walked over the snow-crusted sidewalk on his way to Barbara's house. He had once thought that this was what he wanted but now he felt trapped. Every night of the week! Christ, how had he gotten into this situation? A steady girl was nice to have but this was too steady—he hardly had time to go out and get drunk anymore. How do you tell someone you don't want them anymore? He had tried in the past; he would try again tonight.

The snow crunched under his feet, the night was crisp, and he was tired. He hoped he would be able to get away early, and get to bed…or get to bed early and get home. He smiled and shook his head. No chance, not with Barbara. He'd try though. It never hurt to try. Forget that. He must finish this thing tonight. How many times had he decided that? He should be in bed right now. His mother had been nagging him about staying out so late. He always got up to go to work on time, though.

His father never bothered him about it. He even suspected that his father was proud of the fact he was always staying out so late with Barbara. *The old man thinks I'm humping her,* he thought. "Leave the kid alone," his father would often say to his mother when the subject came up as it so often did. But his mother's persistence was getting to him. With his father, it was different. His decisions would almost always come with a swiftness that defied argument—sometimes with fury and rage and sometimes with just an abrupt yes, no, or short definite answer.

But, Bill never felt himself to be on firm enough ground to try arguing or reason. He had seen his father many times in a fit of uncontrolled temper, and although his father never hit him, he was always threatening to knock Bill "into the middle of next week." His father's decisions were easy enough to maneuver around. Often the old man would forget what his ever-changing rule declarations were, and even if, on a rare occasion, Bill did get caught in disobedience, the punishment was only remembering to withstand the rage without question or argument.

His mother's nagging was getting to him, though. *She will never quit,* Bill thought. Women were like that. Always pretending to be weak and helpless and have no power while they squeezed the life out of you. Bill shook his head and smiled. And, all the while they're doing it, you feel sorry for treating them like you do. He realized that two females were pulling at him, and although they were pulling in opposite directions, both were winning.

VI

"You don't love me, anymore," Barbara said as she turned away and stared blankly at the opposite wall.

Whaddaya mean "anymore"? Bill thought, putting his hands on her shoulders. "Honey, of course I love you, I just think that when two people love each other… when they are young—well, if they see other people as well, that will just make their love more meaningful." *It's not going to go,* Bill thought.

Barbara started crying. She turned to him sniffing and swallowing her sobs. "I… I don't see how your seeing someone like—like that whore you went out with once—will make you love me more."

Bill shook his head. "We agreed that was done with, and we wouldn't mention it again."

"Well, you're the one who wants to go out with other girls. What am I supposed to think?"

"Nothing." Bill sat down on the sofa, swung his feet around, and lay back on the pillows. He closed his eyes and tried to quiet his thoughts during the silence that hung as heavy as fog.

"And…and, I suppose you want to go out and get drunk every night with your-your buddies."

Bill closed his mind to her outburst having decided that ignoring her was the best way to both punish her and shut her up.

It seemed to take her longer than usual, but she finally started in like Bill knew she would. How many times would she say she was sorry between the sobs, the kissing, and sniffing at her running nose. Bill had once decided that he would count them and this time he had even started, but, like always, he got caught up in the continuous necking, and he could feel the heat rising in his body, as she lay beside him, her body pressing and rubbing against his, as they kissed and squeezed and occasionally sobbed. *Maybe tonight she will let me,* Bill thought, knowing that she wouldn't and fearing that she would.

Bill often wondered if her mother listened to their arguments and then their renewed passions from her bedroom upstairs. The old lady sure gives us the opportunity Bill thought—too bad her daughter is not as accommodating.

Barbara's father would often come home about one or two, after getting out of work at nine. At first, Bill had insisted on getting up from the sofa, his hair tousled and his face red, but Barbara had always ignored her father or else asked him a question like "drunk as usual?" and eventually Bill learned to ignore him too, and it was hardly even an interruption in their necking as the old man went grumbling up the stairs.

The nightly frustrations of unfulfilled desires and monotonous daily routine of working in a parking lot was getting to Bill. Bill's parents, his friends, even her parents, he guessed, thought he was humping her. "What's the difference?" he asked one time bolting upright from the sofa after she had clamped down on his wrist for the thirty-third time in the last five minutes.

"You don't love me," she said with a sob, as she turned away and stared blankly at the opposite wall.

* * *

Bill stared at the three empty glasses which lay in front of him on the table. He looked at his watch. He had waited for half an hour, and he had made up his mind to accept what a part of him had known from the start—she wasn't coming back. He was both angry and relieved but, more than anything else, he was depressed. By this time, the Petty Officer's Club had filled up and the sounds of music, loud talking, and laughter poured from the nearby cocktail area. Bill considered joining the crowd, but he knew that there was no way that he could really join them. *They're probably all skimmers, anyway,* he thought. He paid his check and got his coat—he had checked two coats on the same ticket but, not surprisingly, the girl only returned with one—he didn't even ask about it.

He walked back out into the cloudy night and slowly wandered, as he watched the many sailors hurriedly moving here and there with their drunkenness and their women. You pay for both, Bill thought, and loneliness often makes both depressing. He picked up his pace and headed for the nearest bar. He resolved that he would get drunk and get laid and do both as quickly and cheaply as possible.

VII

Bill hadn't wanted to get up the next morning, but he had duty and had to go on watch. His head hurt, his body hurt, and the bruises and cuts on his face hurt when he touched them. At first, he didn't remember what had happened, but after he became fully awake and aware, he remembered too well and wished that he couldn't. He wasn't interested in breakfast and, as he headed back aft to take the watch, he ignored the people who either winced when they looked at him or asked him what happened.

When he arrived back in maneuvering, Parsons was already sitting at one of the panels. "What happened? You cut yourself shaving?" he asked as he gave his customary cackle.

Bill had a momentary urge to take a swing at him, but he seldom acted on impulse and this was no exception. "It was those shore patrol, or I think it was the same ones. They beat me up just for having my coat open."

"Couldn't have been for anything you said?" Parsons asked still laughing.

"Yeah, maybe," Bill said sitting down at a panel next to Parsons. "Yeah, maybe."

"You really did get fucked. Did anyone take care of ya?"

"Yeah."

"Yeah, me too." Parsons said.

There was very little further conversation, as both men sat staring more inward than outward.

Bill's urge to strike out against Parsons had been only momentary. He realized that beneath the who-gives-a-damn exterior there was a person who really wanted to be his friend and who had an honest concern for him. He was ashamed for his feelings of not wanting Parsons along the previous evening. He had felt that Parsons would cheapen his experience. This same feeling had been reflected in his attitude of being willing and even desirous of paying a lot for his treasure.

He remembered what Parsons had said when he half-heartedly asked him along—that he was not finished drinking yet. What he meant, Bill now knew, was that he had not yet been drunk enough to use a girl who didn't really want him. He would never admit this Bill thought, and then he realized what Parsons saw in him as a friend—with Bill, he didn't have to.

Bill wondered if Parsons knew some of his secrets too, and he guessed that he probably did. He knew about Noreco Bill thought. He could have told me outright, but he knew that, even if he had, it wouldn't have made any difference in what happened; it just would have made him embarrassed, uneasy, and even resentful toward Parsons afterwards.

He probably figured it was a good lesson. Parsons was like that—he often showed an irritating outward enjoyment at watching people learn what he already knew. And Bill guessed that probably a cardinal rule in Parsons's game was never to obviously forewarn. Bill knew that if the other men on the boat found out what happened to him with Noreco that he would hear about it forever, and he was grateful that Parsons didn't probe him about it. He felt a certain trust of Parsons that he had not had before and even figured that eventually he would be willing to talk with him about his experiences with Noreco—

probably even laugh about it. There was one thing, though, that he didn't figure to ever let anyone know about, and that was how he had gotten beaten up.

Even Parsons, especially Parsons, would be unable to contain himself if he knew that the last girl Bill had picked up had beat him with an ashtray after he had puked all over her in the hotel room.

Chapter X

We are the boys from Wonderland
And we know that we are grand
We make your water and electricity
We brew the steam that makes us go
From Naha to Sasabo
And that's the reason why we draw P-3

—Radio Station N-U-K-E.

The first couple of days after leaving Naha were different in Bill's experience. The crewmembers recuperated from their hangovers and lack of sleeps and spent much of their time recounting their exploits. Bill didn't say much, but he couldn't help being caught up in the atmosphere, and he too began to look to the next liberty port as embodying a true source of future fun.

He recalled when he was a boy of nine or ten, casting his hope for happiness first on one future event and then, after passing, on to the next, never really stopping to take account of the fact that it was the hope itself, not the initially submerged mountains from which the lava of anticipation rose, that had kept his feet dry.

He remembered one event that had been the cause of more than the usual amount of anticipation. He had formulated the feeling that if he lived long enough to experience 'bottle cap' day at the amusement park, his life would be complete, and it wouldn't matter if he died the next day. Looking back on many events, he realized that he remembered most vividly the hope and the wanting but the actual event itself took little shape in his memory. This thing too changed, as he relied less on the satisfaction gained from anticipation, and more on the reality of actual experiences. The concrete forms of past happenings stayed on as both welcome and unwanted guests. This often led or pushed him whenever he slackened his grip on his strong determination of spirit that had all but completely taken the place of island hopping on pieces of hope.

It would be only six days after leaving Naha that they would arrive in Sasabo, Japan. The plan was to stay there for seven days, over the Christmas holiday, and then move into a two-month patrol. The crew would be paid in advance, upon arriving in Sasabo. Most married and a few single men planned to send most of their money home, and some did not. Almost everyone, though, had intentions of taking advantage of the cheap navy exchange prices and sending home many late Christmas gifts. This was the second thing that most of the men intended to attend to after arriving in port.

Of course, all the crew members professed to have good intentions, but one person in particular seemed to have a capacity for proclaiming more than most. Every established crew member on board was recognized by some distinguishing trait and with Dave McGrew, alias "Dirty Dan," it was talking. McGrew was a verbal champion on causes, and he had once argued for an entire four-hour watch with Parsons about the rightful role of the negro in society. His most frequent and apparently favorite subject, however, was the navy, most specifically the nuclear navy, and what it was doing to people in general and his body in particular. As a "nuke" crew member, he looked upon himself as both elite and oppressed.

He often expounded on the history of how he had gotten entrapped in the seven-year nuclear maze (six-year enlistment and one extra to qualify for pro pay), and he expressed the desire to serve as a recruiter, so he could give the "straight skinny" with no bullshit.

McGrew did not have an ordinary "nuke" job aboard the boat. He was an R.O. (reactor operator), a position which required extra training, extra time to qualify, and extra duty time once qualified. McGrew and Parsons were the only qualified R.O.s on board. This position afforded him the opportunity to stand all his watches in maneuvering at the reactor plant control panel (RPCP).This was his podium where he verbalized for hours on end about what was not right with the world in general and his world in particular.

To the unsophisticated ear, McGrew was regarded as a bitcher and complainer and the chief in charge of the R.O.s had once offered to trade him for a bent shit-can lid. Bill, however, at first regarded him as truly a person with principles, but after experiencing many hours of just talk, he came to think of him as just a good entertainer.

During one watch, when Bill was standing the SPCP, McGrew was quiet for almost the first two hours, and this, undoubtedly, would have seemed strange to Bill had he not been lost in his own thoughts about what it would be like in the upcoming liberty port of Sasabo.

All the maneuvering watch standers, including the E00W and EPCP operators were being unusually quiet, possibly enjoying the change from the typical McGrew manned watch area, and time was passing slowly but not unbearably so.

Even the presence of the AEA did not disturb the quiet, and no one bothered even to goose him when he came into maneuvering to take his readings from the temperature monitoring panels.

It would have been unusual had the entire watch period passed without some BS but, surprisingly, it was not McGrew who charted the course of the conversation.

"Did you hear the yeoman's tapes?" Steve Delay, the EPCP operator, asked speaking to no one in particular. DeLay, unlike McGrew, was known and well respected for his actions rather than his words. He had been aboard less time than Bill but one of his exploits shortly after arriving had elevated him to hero status and created a legend that would survive long after he departed the boat.

He had traveled down to San Louise, Mexico with five other crewmembers and, in the space of one evening as partially verified by his compatriots, purchased the pleasures of seven young women. He claimed it was his insatiable need, and the open option of available fare that caused him to "thrash" beyond the agreed to time limit that all were to meet at the car for the return to San Diego.

His partners waited up until the time they could wait no longer and still make it back for muster the next morning, and then they left him figuring him to be in jail, not in the arms of another flame of the night. When he did show up at the meeting place and found no means of transportation, he did the only logical thing—he chartered a plane. The fact that he had only a couple of dollars didn't deter him, and he showed up at the boat with a taxi driver and a pilot both waiting for him to borrow the money for their payment. After that, he was known as "Super Thrash," and he was heroized by everyone except for the person who had loaned him the money and had not yet gotten it back.

"Yeah, I heard those tapes," McGrew said, "and I've been thinking a lot about it.

"What tapes"? Bill asked.

"The ones that were played during soup call, "McGrew said. "That goddamned Huffman is bitching about nukes again."

"So, what's new," Bill asked. What's his complaint about this time?"

"Oh, he made some stupid skit about the nukes spilling coffee in front of his office and not wiping it up," DeLay said.

"His real gripe is the fact that we draw pro-pay and he doesn't, though."

"So, let him gripe," Bill said. "Who listens to him?"

"That's not the point," McGrew said. "Besides, there are plenty like him. You can't even go forward any more without one of those noseconers running off at the mouth about the *goddamned nukes*."

"Yeah, know what you mean," DeLay said. "And the yeoman is the worst of the lot of them."

Lieutenant Welty, the RDOW, put down the RPM he was reading. "I heard that tape," he said, "and I thought it was pretty good. The yeoman has a way with words."

"Like hell," McGrew said. "He's got no imagination; he doesn't know how to capture an audience."

"He got *your* attention," Welty said.

"He just pissed me off," McGrew said.

"That's what he was trying to do," Bill said, thinking about how often Parsons would laugh at whatever was McGrew's consternation of the moment.

"Oh, it wasn't what he did or even how he did it," McGrew said. "It's the whole goddamned attitude that's behind it. We must live together and work together for a good long time, and we should be figuring out ways to make things easier. Enough bickering will come later, after we've been at sea for several months and tempers are really frazzled."

"Well, why don't you figure something out," Welty asked.

"Whaddaya mean?" McGrew asked.

"I mean you talk a lot McGrew, but that's all you ever do. You say someone should figure out something to improve morale and you complain that the yeoman did the opposite. Well, he improved my morale. I thought he was pretty good."

Bill expected McGrew to really get excited over Welty's baiting, but he didn't.

McGrew didn't say anything for a moment, and then he said in a low voice as if he were talking to himself, "Maybe you're right; perhaps that approach does have some potential.

And then in a louder voice looking at Welty, he said, "Sometimes talk *is* action."

"What are you going to do?" Bill asked, feeling himself to be almost in on something and not understanding what it was.

"You ever been insulted so good that you had to take it as a joke, because you couldn't adequately fight back with words of your own?"

"You think you can shut the yeoman up by making him laugh?"

"Well, if I can't do better than Huffman with words, then I'll be the one who'll shut up."

"That almost makes me want to pull for Huffman," Welty said.

"Hey, that's good," McGrew said. "That is the kind of thing I'm talking about. DeLay, you have your guitar on board. don't you? Look, if you play the music and be the straight man I can do a far-out disc jockey bit and—hand me a pencil and paper, will you? And I'll lay this thing out."

* * *

The next day, there was a broadcast over the entertainment speakers in the crew's mess:

(DeLay)

This is radio station N-U-K-E covering all of Sculpin at 69 mega-cycles on your dial and 78 mega-watts of soul power. This broadcast is coming to you straight from the heart of the money belt, aft of frame 44. Now, we will turn the mike over to our famous millionaire D.J., Big Daddy Greenbacks.

(McGrew)

Hot Dog! Baby! We're gonna start the show right off with a bang. I know ya gonna like this one cause it is the station theme song – MONEY!!

(DeLay)

The best things in life are free
But they don't compare to 'P-3'
I need money—that's what I want
Some of that genius pay. Give me
Money, yeah. Give me money
Money don't buy everything, it's true
But I can buy a lot more than you
I need money. Yeah. P-3
Give me money
Just a hundred a month, give me
Money. Yeah, give me money
Your bitching gives me such a thrill
But your bitching don't pay my
Bills. I need money, yeah, give
Me money. I need a hundred a month
Give me money yeah, give me money
Just a hundred a month, give me money
Well, I want P-3, give me money
I went to school a year, give me money
Well, that's what I want to hear
Give me money. Yeah, give me money

(McGrew)

Whooo-ee, Baby! Don't that song make your wallet just want
to jump and shout? It's just toooo much.

(DeLay)

Listen friends; are you one of those poor unfortunates who's
not making the most of his earning power? Do you scrimp and
sweat from payday to payday? If so, Big Daddy's got some
words to lay on your bod.

(McGrew)

Hot Dog, Baby! I've got a money back offer for you; it won't cost you one thin dime. Just drop a quarter, or fourth of a dollar, in an un-va-lope along with your name and bunk number, and we gonna send to you absolutely free a copy of that eye-opening how to make coin book entitled, How to Become a Nuke Genius and Draw P-3.

Yeah, friends, if you are tired of that unchallenging job of pounding a typewriter or der-riving the bus, this is the book for you. Hot Dog, Baby! You gonna make lots of money after reading this publication. It contains such chapters as, The Slide Rule for Fun and Profit, The Neutron and You, and It Only Takes a Year to Become a Genius. This is just a small sample of the information contained in this book. All you cats can become financial tigers.

Remember, it won't cost you a dime, just drop off your quarter along with your name and bunk number in the maneuvering area, and we'll send you this boss book.

Hot Dog, Baby! Now we gonna get back to re-corded sooooul music. This one is by the king, the big boss, the only cat who qualifies for Peeeeeee-5-Supa! Therrash! Yee-ow, work out, Baby!

(DeLay)

Well, we are the boys from wonderland, and we know that we are grand. We make your water and electricity.

We brew the steam that makes you go from Naha to Sasabo, and that's the reason why we draw P-3.

So, listen here you forward pukes, the reason there are nukes—just open up your eyes and you'll see, the reason there are nukes is so all you forward pukes can get yourselves some goddamned liberty.

(McGrew)

Ain't that the way it is, Baby! Hot Dog!

(DeLay)

And now it's time for radio station N-U-K-E's ever popular program on which we present unusual personalities to our listening audience, The In-Corner. Today our guest is someone we all know but, unfortunately, do not admire – Nubbie Noseconer.

Hello Nubbie, welcome to the In Corner. We would like you to fill our audience in on what you do on board a nuclear submarine.

(3rd crew-member)

Well … I eat a lot, sleep most of the time, and use up a lot of air.

(DeLay)

You mean that's all you have to do?

(3rd crew-member)

What did ya expect? I don't draw P-3. Sometimes, I'm forced into planes' watch if there aren't enough nukes around to do it, and, occasionally, I have to type a little too.

(DeLay)

Oh, you type? You probably have to type pretty fast to keep up with all that important correspondence.

(3rd crew-member)

Yeah, that's right, in fact, I'm so fast I can let it all stack up for a couple of weeks and then do it all at once. I mean, after all, when you can type five words a minute, it's no sweat.

(DeLay)

Wow! I bet it took a long time to learn how to do all those things. You must be pretty smart.

(3rd crew-member)

Well, can't say I am and can't say I ain't. I don't like to brag but those two weeks of yeoman school were really rough for most guys.

(DeLay)

You say most guys, Nubbie. Wasn't it rough for you?

(3rd crew-member)

Not really, I was the smartest guy in the class. My G.C.T. (aptitude test administered upon joining the navy—average score is 50) is '3'.

(DeLay)

Well, Nubbie, it's been nice talking to you today. We know it's drawing close to the time to make out the P.O.D., so we won't detain you any longer.

(3rd crew-member)

Thanks a lot. I do have to go, but not to make out the plan of the day. There's a hot poker game down in the crew's mess. I'll do the P.O.D. at six o'clock in the morning—just before the XO gets up.

(DeLay)

Goodbye, Nubbie. I'm sure our audience has enjoyed hearing your story. I'd like to say I wish you luck in the poker game. I understand you need the money.

That concludes today's program from the In-Corner, now back to Big Daddy Greenbacks for more recorded soul.

(McGrew)

Hot Dog, Baby! Ain't that Nubbie Noseconer some kind of different. This next one I'm going to send out especially for him. Take it away Supa' Ther-rash!

(DeLay)

My bills are all paid, so I'm going to get laid
I get pro-pay
Liberty's down in Naha town
I get pro-pay
I've got greenbacks a heap, so I'll go get a leap
You poor ol' noseconers will stay here and weep
But just don't you worry, we'll sail in a week
I get pro-pay
You go to the slush fund to ask for a loan, you
Get no-pay
The chief of the boat has done packed up and gone
He got your pay
You poor ol' noseconers have a hard row to hoe
But don't talk to me, just go cry with the yeo
It's not my fault if your IQ's too low
I get pro-pay

(McGrew)

Ain't that boss, Baby! It's just the ultimate! Hot Dog! This is the most powerful mobile radio station in the world: N-U-K-E, with

78 mega-watts of pure sooooul power, coming to you straight from the heart of the money belt aft of frame 44. Cats, Big Daddy is going to have to move along now. If you have been digging Big Daddy, drop me a line and let me know. Send it to radio station N-U-K-E care of the maneuvering room. And friends, don't send no prayer cards. I've got enough troubles of my own. Hot Dog, Baby!

This is radio station N-U-K-E signing off.

(DeLay)

The best things in life are free
But they don't compare to P-3
I need money ….

Chapter XI

Mirroring movements I sense in your mind
Leaving my thoughts and my choices behind
We're dancing to music that neither can find
I'll follow your deal and you follow mine

—Bill

I

When Bill assumed the next SPCP watch, Parsons had not yet been relieved from the previous R.O watch.

"I thought you were supposed to be relived two hours ago," Bill said.

"Yeah, well McGrew will have to make it up later. He's up talking to the old man."

"He's been talking to him for two hours?"

"Dunno, could be. But you know how that goes. If the captain wants to talk to you, he wants you available in a certain spot when he gets around to it. He could be waiting, or he could be talking to him. If the old man is pissed at him, you can bet he made him wait, though."

"You think he might be angry about the tape?"

"Could be. He's funny like that. The cob told me he was getting all bent out of shape about the poker games. Word is that if we don't keep the money off the table, he's going to shut the games off."

"Why would he be jacked up about the tape? You know anything, Mr. Welty?"

"I think he liked them. He sure laughed a lot when he heard them, anyway. He may be concerned that they may cause some hostility, however. Right after, he called Mr. Brown into his stateroom, and Mr. Brown was in there for more than an hour."

"Did he talk to him as the navigation officer, the morale officer, or the Catholic lay leader?" Bill asked.

"Who knows," Welty said. "I haven't talked to Brown since, and the captain didn't see fit to fill me in. It's hard to believe, but sometimes he just doesn't tell me everything."

"Well, I don't care who he tells what to," Parsons said, "but if he doesn't let McGrew stand his watch, he can come back here and take this watch. According to the schedule, I'm supposed to be back on watch in another four hours. Well, I may be still here then to relieve myself."

"You're not letting them get to you, are you Frank?" Bill asked, patting him on the thigh.

"Before they get to me, I'll get off this tub. I can always go to the hospital. When I went over to Balboa Hospital in San Diego, that doctor said that my problem was my nerves."

"I thought you had an ulcer?"

"They couldn't find one. He asked me about my job, and I told him. He asked me if I wanted off."

"So, how come you're still here?"

"I figured that since the navy has fit me this long, if I go, the time has to be right."

"Whaddaya mean," Bill asked.

"I've been on this boat almost four years, and during that time, I've lost leave because I've been too valuable to let go. They cancelled my shore duty orders twice, because they said there was no one to take my place. They automatically changed me from I.C. electrician to E.T. (electronics technician), but they denied my request to go to 'A' school so I could learn enough to make first class. Did I ever tell you what Wagner did to me?"

"Yeah, you told me," Bill said, knowing he was about to hear it again.

"That son-of-a-bitch gave me weekend leave to travel to Bremerton to get my car back down to San Diego after we left the yard up there. Then he tried to bust me because I was six hours late. The old man wouldn't go along with it, though. Wagner told me I'd never get another day's leave as long as he was on the boat, and I haven't either. So, if I go, it has to be when they need me the most, and that could be anytime."

"Alright, turn it off, Parsons," Welty said. "The reason you're in the shits all the time is because you don't know when to keep your mouth shut. If the X.O. heard you, he'd have your ass."

"Wagner wouldn't do shit," Parsons said. "There are only two qualified R.O.s on here, and I'm one of them. It takes a year to qualify another R.O. and no one's even close. Even if one does get qualified before we get back, McGrew's getting out then, so it's the same old story. You guys fuck with me any more than you have already, and it's the EOOWs who will be on back to back, because they would also have to take turns taking an R.O. watch. And that wouldn't work either, because the only officer on here that would know who to handle it would be the engineer."

Welty didn't say anything.

II

Sometimes, Bill would see things as if each moment were slowed down to a crawling pace and smoothly and continuously connected to the next. No longer would individual happenings seem disjointed or words seem out of place.

Characters would do whatever they did and say whatever they said and the whole process seemed to have a perpetual motion that fed upon itself alone.

He didn't will himself to see things as he did, and he often wondered if others found themselves as a momentary separated observer. It was a common thing to hear other people say that they liked to watch people, but they always said it with a smugness that purported a certain choice and superiority. Seeing things as he did, did not make Bill feel superior, instead it caused a feeling of sadness that he could partially perceive something he could not control. Also, it was in knowing that he himself sometimes acted to be compatible with his anticipated perception of how others saw him that caused a feeling of loneliness in relation to the part of him that he felt may be waiting to turn a different corner.

"—morale booster. He said that laughter could do a lot to bring the crew together and make time go faster."

Bill refocused his attention on McGrew. "It took him two and a half hours to tell you that?" he asked.

"Well, we talked about a lot of things." McGrew said. "He talked to Huffman, too. He wants us to get together on an entertainment program."

"You and Huffman?" Welty said.

"Yas-zoo, Boss," McGrew said. Huffman's okay and us working together will allow him to regain the status he lost. He's smart enough to know that and big enough not to be bitter about it."

"Even the noseconers gave him a hard time after that tape," added DeLay, who was sitting at the RPCP anc said nothing up to this point.

"You going to continue the radio station format," Bill asked.

"The captain thought that was a good idea," McGrew said. "We need another theme, though. One for the whole crew. That's one of the reasons he wanted Huffman in on it The nuke thing was good for only a one-shot deal."

"You got anything figured out?" Welty asked.

"Not yet, but whatever it is, it'll have to be something most everyone can identify with."

"You being on back to back doesn't give you much time to work on it," Bill said.

"The old man said I could work on it while on watch," McGrew said. "He said that this could be a special case." He looked at Welty and nodded toward DeLay. "He said when DeLay and I are together, that he could work with me."

"Just make sure you keep one eye on your panels," Welty said shaking his head.

"Yas-zoo, Boss," McGrew said stretching back in his chair and staring in the direction of the control panel. "It has to be something especially unique to submarine sailors," he mused.

Welty looked up from the manual that he had started to read, "Huh?"

"The theme," McGrew said. "Goddamn, Mr. Welty, for an officer you sure are drifty."

"He's drifty because he's an officer," DeLay said.

III

When Bill got off watch, he checked Parsons's bunk and, when he didn't find him there, he went back up to the crew's mess, got a cup, filled it with ice, and headed down to the storeroom.

Parsons didn't say anything when Bill came in and sat down on a container. Bill held out his cup and Parsons filled it up.

"You figure to stay in?" Bill asked.

Parsons tipped his cup up until it was empty and then refilled it. "My time isn't up for another year," he said.

"I know," Bill said. "Are you sorry you extended for pro-pay?"

"Nope," Parsons looked Bill straight in the eye. "Don't be sorry for nothing," he said. "Doesn't change anything."

"Maybe not," Bill said. "But wouldn't you want to be getting out now?"

"Nope, I can wait."

"How come you did Welty like that? He can shit on you, you know."

"We understand each other," Parsons said.

"Were you really serious about going to the hospital?"

"Wouldn't have said it if I wasn't."

"You mean you figure to try it?"

"Dunno. Might."

Bill took a long drink, and grimaced as he put the cup down.

"So, it doesn't make much since to tell them you're planning it."

"That's the only way I'd do it," Parsons said holding out the bottles.

Bill put his hand over the top of the cup. "No more," he said. "When you gotta go back on watch?"

"McGrew is supposed to call forward when he expects to be relieved."

"They may have to look for you if you're not in your bunk."

"So, I might be a little late," Parsons said, taking another drink."

"If they find out you've been drinking, you might not have a choice about leaving."

Parsons smiled and took another drink. "I'm not the only one on here that has a bottle or two stashed, and they know it. I'm the last one they'll catch at it, though." Parsons said winking. "Let me tell you something, Bill. It's no fun getting away with something if no one knows about it."

"What are you going to do when you get out?" Bill asked.

"I guess I'll go to the University of Arkansas." Parsons said. "What are you going to do?"

"I figure to go to college too. I've got to get out. I didn't even extend for pro-pay. I don't like it," Bill said shaking his head.

"I do," Parsons said.

Bill looked at him. "Then why?"

"Because they're trying to do me," Parsons said.

Bill looked at Parsons a moment and then understood. "You ever consider going back with your ex-wife," he asked.

"I sent her flowers once," he said, "on her birthday." Parsons laughed. "I know she cried when she got them. She's like that. I didn't sign the card, but she'd know they were from me."

"Yeah, I guess she would. You think you'll ever get married again?"

"A person who makes the same mistake twice deserves what he gets," Parsons said.

Bill got up to leave. "Well, I'm going to hit the sack for a while. You ought to get some sleep, too."

"I was going to, but I had to settle my stomach first. It's too late now."

"What are you going to do?"

"Guess, I'll go up in the crew's mess and see if I can catch the tail end of the soup call. Don't worry; I'll put the bottle away. Who needs a wife when you're around to look out for me."

"Yeah, right." Bill laughed an awkward laugh and turned to walk away.

"Bill?"

He turned back to face Parsons. "Yeah?"

"When we hit Sasabo, let's go to the beach together."

"Okay," Bill said, "but one thing."

Parsons finished his drink and stood up, picking up his bottle. "What's that?"

"I'm not heading toward the hospital," Bill said.

"You don't even know where it is," Parsons said.

"Yes, I do." Bill said walking away.

IV

Bill didn't go right to sleep. Instead, for some reason, his thoughts turned to his high school days. And finally, when he did sleep, his dreams took over and reshaped the thoughts into an actual event which he had always resisted thinking about, but which now he was re-living. An event that happened when he was in high school:

* * *

Why would he want to be *his* friend, Bill wondered as he watched the boy who was walking with the other boy everyone called "Captain Vogel." Bill didn't know why he was called that or why other boys teased him, but the boy Bill had been with the previous day had amused himself by pushing between those same two boys several times, and now, without even considering why, Bill would do it.

Bill increased his pace until he caught up with the boys. While walking close behind them, he sized them up. Of the two, "Captain Vogel" was the taller. He had red curly hair and a freckled babyish face. The other boy was slightly taller than Bill and stockier than his companion. His hair was straight and dark. Bill had seen him around school—he was a grade ahead of him. He had heard him called "Warren." Bill deliberately took note, with a certain sense of satisfaction, that both boys were bigger and older than he was. He told himself that this made a difference, and he would not do what he was going to do had this not been so. Moving ahead faster, Bill pushed between the boys. "Out of my way," he said.

"Hey! Watch it," Warren said.

Bill stopped and turned. "You guys are taking up the whole sidewalk," he said. "You ought to leave room for someone to get by."

"Just don't do it again," Warren said. The red-haired boy said nothing and didn't even look Bill in the eye.

Bill walked ahead. At first, he thought he would leave them alone after he had bothered them once, but Warren's seemingly challenging warning worked in his mind until he crossed the street and dropped back.

He sensed that they knew he was coming when he pushed through the second time, but they didn't get out of the way; instead, after he crashed through, they stopped and waited for Bill to face them. So deliberate was this re-action that Bill figured they must have planned it.

Bill didn't even think about not stopping. He half expected Warren to swing at him as he turned around, but he didn't try to defend against this possibility. He could take it if it came. He would handle what came after.

"I told you not to do that," Warren said with his fists clenched.

"Yeah, I heard you," Bill said. "I just wanted to see if you meant it." He made no threatening or defensive gestures; he just waited.

The taller boy finally spoke. "C'mon, Warren, let's go. Don't let him push you into anything."

"You do it again, and I'll make you sorry," Warren said. He intended to accent his warning by staring at Bill for another moment, but Bill moved toward him. At first, he didn't seem to be sure what Bill's advance meant, but then, noticing that Bill's arms still hung loosely, he realized that Bill was challenging him, not attacking. The boy held firm as their shoulders met, and he pushed Bill away and held his fists up. "Alright, if it's a fight you want, c'mon."

"Me? Want a fight?" Bill said. "I'm not the one who threatened to make someone 'sorry', and what's the idea of pushing me?" He reached out to push at Warren.

Bill didn't complete his motion, however, for Warren's fist shot out and smashed against the side of his cheek.

As Bill staggered back, the red-haired boy turned and ran. Warren stood waiting with his fists still before his face.

Bill walked into a left hook, which thudded against the side of his right eye. This was followed by a right, which smashed into his nose. Blood dripped from his left nostril. Warren again remained waiting.

Bill rubbed the back of his hand across his upper lip. He looked at the blood. "I'll get you for that," he said.

Bill slowly sidestepped to the left, staying about the same distance from Warren. His knees were bent, and his arms were extended out with his hands open and fingers separated.

Warren held his fists ready as he turned to follow Bill's circling.

"Go ahead, hit me," Bill said as he jumped at him.

Warren did hit him, but it didn't stop him. Bill grabbed Warren and wrestled him to the ground. Warren struggled to get free, but Bill was too strong for him. Bill pinned him to the ground and still had one hand free to punish him.

Bill slapped him across the face. "You better give up," he said.

"What's a matter? You too yellow to fight fair?" Warren asked.

Bill slapped him again and then got up. "I'll show you who's yellow. Get up!"

Bill stood over Warren until he began to push himself to his feet. He took a step back as Warren started to rise. Just before Warren had gained a full standing position, Bill stepped forward and sent his right fist crashing toward Warren's head. Warren saw it coming, but he was unable to avoid it.

"Now you got him, Bill," a voice shouted as Warren fell back to the ground.

Bill turned to the group of boys that had gathered, and he noticed several familiar faces. Bill's diverted attention gave Warren the chance to get back up.

"Go get him, Bill" someone said.

Bill rushed toward Warren with his right fist cocked back next to his ear.

Warren jabbed with his left and hit Bill in the mouth. Bill's lip split and blood splattered his chin. Bill stood his ground and swung wildly.

Warren ducked under a round-house right, jabbed at Bill's stomach, and then stepped back. Bill charged after him and Warren met him with a right to the eye. Bill lowered his head and swung his fists blindly.

"Lead with your left, Bill. Lead with your left," a voice from the crowd shouted.

Bill stopped. His arms hung down to his sides and his chest rose and fell with deep breaths. His face was cut and swollen, and from his nose and lip, red splotches of blood dripped onto his shirt.

"Had enough?" Warren asked.

"I'll show you," Bill said as he started after Warren again.

Warren backed away, ducking or blocking Bill's wild swings and continually shooting out sharp jabs that opened new cuts on Bill's bruised face.

Bill stumbled, falling on his hands and knees. Warren stood watching him, unwilling to pursue his advantage. "Why don't you give in? I don't want to hurt you," he said.

Bill pushed himself to his feet and stood with his hands on his knees drawing deep breaths.

"I told you he was going to lose," someone said.

Bill took a deep breath and jumped from his crouched position toward Warren. Warren was not prepared for Bill's lunge and his step backward wasn't quick enough to avoid Bill's extended arms and only threw him off balance. He crashed to the ground and Bill landed on top of him. The fall knocked the wind out of Warren, and he was unable to offer any resistance as Bill seated himself on his chest with his knees on his arms.

Warren struggled for breath. "…not…not fair," he said.

If Bill heard at all, he ignored him. He grabbed Warren by the hair with his left hand and began slapping him across the face with his right. The slaps cracked loudly as Bill connected first with the back of his hand and then with his palm. Blood bubbled out of the corner of Warren's mouth as he tried to protest. "Don't…. not fair… stop…."

"Kill him, Bill. Kill him!" a voice shouted.

Bill suddenly became fully aware of the crowd that had closed in around them. A ring of faces was hanging over him. One boy was pounding his fist into his hand. Bill felt that he could feel their breath on the back of his neck, and he shivered.

"Smash him again, Bill. Smash him," a voice yelled.

Bill felt sick. He slowly got up and started walking away. Some of the boys from the crowd followed him, and one of the boys put his hand on Bill's shoulder. "Aw, you sure let him off easy Bill."

Bill wanted to run, to be away from what had happened, but he didn't. And he shut out of his mind the thoughts that were uncomfortable. He accepted the boy's arm on his shoulder, and he smiled weakly and said nothing.

Bill was not surprised by his father's reaction upon seeing his face. He didn't ask why he had been fighting or even admonish him for doing it. Only, "Who won?" And when he was satisfied with the answer, he said no more.

Bill had the badge of the brawl written on his face for several weeks, and he was soon ready with quick remarks to fire back at the joking comments like, "You oughta see the other guy."

Of course, the story spread at school, and when Warren returned to school with a bandaged finger, which he had broken on Bill's face, it became easier to rationalize that Warren had gotten the worst of it.

Bill often saw Warren at school, and they would always nod to each other. Bill sensed that Warren had a certain respect for him. At any rate, there was no resentment between them. He also saw the tall red-haired boy occasionally, but he never again called him "Captain Vogel," and when he did recognize him, Bill avoided looking him in the eyes.

* * *

As Bill drifted through half-sleep into wakefulness, his thoughts also changed from re-experience to remembering. And, when he was fully aware that he was consciously remembering, Bill was, for the first time, able to acknowledge the shame in what he had done. He realized that it was only one short occurrence in his life, but it was one that he would not hide in the back of his mind again, for in its clarity, it represented all the smaller happenings that would never be fully remembered but nevertheless a part of him, and Bill hoped, were not, and would not be, the larger part.

Bill tried to remember more about the boy whom he had first seen antagonize Warren and "Captain Vogel" but he couldn't. He realized that he had never considered this boy a friend, and he wasn't even someone he had looked up to. This seemed funny in a way, yet he felt he understood, and this awareness helped him understand how he got to the man he was now. He both regretted and, strangely, appreciated the path he had traveled to get there.

Chapter XII

If you call me a queer
I'll kick your rear
And throw you in the drink
But call me a pre-vert
And I'll kiss your ear
And throw you a little wink
–Condensed philosophy –

—Radio S.T.U.D.

Looking from the outside
Is like looking through a hue
Which colors and distorts things
And shows things less than true
But when looking from the inside
We sometimes see too pure
So, we color and distort things
Just so we can endure

—Liam

(McGrew)

Hello out there in radio land, welcome to station S-T-U-D, the radio station designed and originated with the crew of the U.S.S. Sculpin in mind. Radio station S-T-U-D operates at seven and one-half inches per second on your machine with a peak output of – Sixty-Nine! Hot Dog, Baby!

Radio station S-T-U-D. is a concerted effort of the committee for the integration of noseconers and nukes.

Radio S-T-U-D, first in news, music, and perrrrrrr-ver-sion, baby! Hot Dog! Today, Big Daddy would like to start the program off with a song dedicated to all the battle-scarred, bedraggled veterans of Naha, Mexico, and San Diego. Take it away, Supa-Ther-rash.

(DeLay)

Silver dolphins on her chest
She's been had by the navy's best
One hundred men, she'll thrash today
But only three in the normal way

Fighting sailors from the deep
Came to thrash and not to sleep
Mighty men with a sailor's lust
They came ashore and thrash they must

She was raised by the sub base gate
Watched her mother stand and wait
Which one's her dad, now no one knows
Not even her mother in her fine silk clothes

She took mom's place in the waiting line
She takes them home, two or three at a time
For her task, she takes no pay
Because she loves the *qualified* way

She'll fill their lust with a wanton rage
Another line in history's page
She learned her trade, and learned it well
God bless her mother—may she rot in hell

When my son's grown, if I'm not here
Just send him down to the sub base pier
The shining dolphins on his chest
Will mark him as the navy's best

He'll stand tall, filled with pride
She'll tremble with lust that she can't hide
She'll take him home, if she still can
Because she loves...a *qualified* man

* * *

Extremely vulnerable to mishap if ever at rest, the submarine never completely ceases forward motion except when tended by a pier or a mother ship. A dark gray blunt shape pushing through the sea, the sub is usually completely submerged. But sometimes, it peeks up on top and occasionally comes up to allow the thin sail to slice through the waves, providing a lookout perch on the sail-planes manned by two watchmen ever ready to jump back within the seal of the thick metal skin, as it quickly slips beneath the surface.

The sea is a heavy cover; it pushes and squeezes, and the creaking of the submarine's thick shell provides a reminder that the sea can crush as well as hide. Inner noise is cushioned by rubber sound mounts that support the rctating machinery, and human noise is muffled by absorbent padding attached to the inner bulkheads. The huge twisting screw is designed for speed and quiet, two attributes which are not completely compatible, and therefore, both are somewhat compromised as the huge blade chops through the dark depths.

It is a small packaged piece of the external world, having its own interrelationship within and, also, having a dependent and two-way influencing, connection without. Not obvious. Designed and coincidental. Smooth and coarse. A world with a seemingly collective single personality.

The inner sub was not completely physically isolated from the liquid that supported it. The cool seawater was taken in and pumped through heat exchangers to condense the steam from the main turbine and the turbine generator's condensers. It also cooled the reactor plant fresh water system which, in turn, cooled the rotating machinery in the reactor compartment. The seawater was then pumped out again with no physical change except for being warmer. And thus, as the sub moved continuously forward, the sea, where it had been, was the same, yet changed by an infinitesimal fraction of a degree of temperature which was obvious more in the minds of the men who knew it than in the ocean that experienced it.

Not continuously, but occasionally, the sub left more to the sea than an unmeasurable warmth, however. The garbage was weighted and expelled, the sanitary tanks were blown out, and even the dirty sea water which leaked from the pumps and valves was pumped back out along with bilge oil, human sweat, and other manufactured liquids purposely or accidently dumped into the bilge.

Subtler than these, however, was the muffled waves of noise which escaped the sound insulation and vibrated out into the surrounding sea.

* * *

(McGrew)

"—like to extend an invitation to any of our listening audience who might have contributions to make in the form of poems, songs, or ideas. We at Radio S-T-U-D are particularly interested in perrrr-ver-sion, baby! But keep it clean. Send any contributions you might have to Station S-T-U-D, care of the ship's office.

(Huffman)

Flash! A news bulletin hot off the line. [The sound of a sound-powered phone in the crew's mess squealed.]

—a major scientific breakthrough to convert peanut shells to shoe leather. It was revealed by a reliable source that the—

* * *

"Hey Niles, turn that down, will ya? The old man just sent word down that it's too loud. Says they're picking it up on their headsets in sonar."

* * *

—this has been another hot news scoop from Radio Station S-T-U-D, first with the news that you should know. Now, back to the studio and Big Daddy.

(McGrew)

Hot Dog, Baby! Be the first in your division to get some peanut shell shoes and some peanut butter socks. Haw! Haw! Elephants just love them and so do hogs. Hot Dog!

Listen here, cats. Big Daddy's got some words to lay on your bod. This is a money-back, yeah, baby, a money-back offer on a brand new product that is some kind of wild. This product is guaranteed, warrantied, and insured to give you everything the designer says it will. You want to know what this product is? Big Daddy got you wondering? Well, hang on to your wazoos there cats. The name of this product is "Doctor Phillips Never-Dull Pills." Now this Doctor Phillips cat is a busy man, but I know him personally and I talked him into coming down and telling you about this product himself. So, c'mon in here Doctor Phillips and tell us about them Never-Dull pills.

(The Ship's Corpsman)

Thanks, Big Daddy, I'm glad you did catch me during a lull in my schedule. My product is really something. I've spent a lot of time perfecting it, and I'd like to tell your listening audience about it.

(McGrew)

Yeah man, our listeners out there in STUD land really gonna dig your bag. Hot Dog! Lay your words on their bods there, Doc, about what your Never-Dull pill does.

(Corpsman)

Are you ready Big Daddy?

(McGrew)

Yeah, Baby!

(Corpsman)

These new Never-Dull capsules make you 'never dull.'

(McGrew)

Oh, ain't that something cats? These Never-Dull pills make you 'never dull'! Uh…how about expounding a little bit on that there, Doc, for the benefit of our listening audience.

(Corpsman)

Well, if you haven't been the talk of your last liberty port, one of these capsules and you soon will be. Take one of these pills before going on liberty and you become an insatiable satyr for about twenty-four hours.

(McGrew)

Hold it Doc. What's this satyr kick, man? Is that some kind of new perversion? Man, that sounds like it might be as neat as the shade of the great pyramid at high noon.

(Corpsman)

Well, Big Daddy, in your language a satyr is a cat whose bag is *sex*—kind of like a male nymphomaniac.

(McGrew)

Hot Dog Baby! That sounds like the stuff for me all right.

(Corpsman)

As I was saying, Big Daddy. These Never-Dulls are great. They make you irresistible to women. And give you that suave, debonair manner. And they bring all those musty old perverted ideas out of your sub-conscious right on up to the surface.

(McGrew)

How long you been working on this stuff, Doc?

(Corpsman)

I'd say roughly about two years. The first human we gave it to, everything became stiff, including his fingers and toes. But, just recently, we obtained the results we've been striving for. This product is now ready for you studs out there.

(McGrew)

Yaz-zoo, Doc! You mean those cats out there are going to get all that for the nominal price of—man, I'm ashamed to say it, it's so ridiculous—sixty-nine cents! Cash, check, or money order. So, you studs out there, get those buffalo bones in the mail, yeah. You don't want to be left behind in Sasabo. And, oh yeah, Doc Phillips says to tell you to take these pills only on liberty days. Otherwise, he will not be held responsible for the pain and perversion you will inflict on your shipmates. Oh yeah! Get those cash, checks, or money orders in to S-T-U-D- and get some Neverrrrr-Dull pills, Yeah, Baby!

* * *

There was a routine developed on the submarine that seemed, upon casual observation, to be automatic. Men ate, slept, stood watches, played poker, and watched movies during the same time periods each twelve hours. The twenty-four-hour day was no longer the unit of routine and the four on, eight off schedule regulated what happened when. Watch sections developed group personalities and men would attempt to shift time periods if their personality and routine did not fit the mode of their current section. The crew's mess was the focal point of each's group activity, and it was important that sections be grouped according to temperament and interests because a poker game and a movie were not compatible.

So that a person would not become too ingrained into the habit-forming routine on one particular watch station, and thus become vulnerable to the unexpected, the watch station within the sections were periodically shifted. The only men who were not shifted from station to station were the men qualified on only one station and the men standing back to back (six on, six off) on a watch station because there was no one to replace them with.

There was much pressure placed on the single station watch standers to induce them to become more functional, but this pressure in no way equaled the squeeze on the no-station men who were expected to quickly be capable of handling part of the load.

These men were seldom in their bunks and quite often were tucked into corners and crannies tracing out pipes and electrical cables or talking to an experienced watch stander about some system or operation.

Each man had gone through this and each man that remained had been successful. In learning to act on the submarine, the sub acted on the man, and this relationship, intense at first, was always working to some degree and, according to interpretation, it was intoxicating, tedious, or agonizing.

* * *

(DeLay)

Well, fifty-two feet beneath the sea
The submarine navy is getting to me
Nuclear power, the wonderland of pre-verts
Pre-verts, pre-verts, pre-verts

Well, under the waves in a leaky ol' boat
Sometimes I wonder how we stay afloat
The chow we get I wouldn't feed a goat
Or pre-verts, pre-verts, pre-verts

Well, the raunchy ol' Sculpin is really not bad
And the crew we got is just great
But I'm telling ya buddy I wouldn't let you
Take my sister out on a date

So, if you join the navy, and you probably will
And you don't want to be just a run-of-the-mill
Just tell your recruiter you want to be a
Submarine
Pre-vert, pre-vert, pre-vert

* * *

Many things affected the submarine's buoyancy and trim. Filling fresh water from the stills, pumping bilges, blowing sanitaries, even crew's mess gatherings for chow and movies had an affect which was, in turn, neutralized by filling or pumping 'forward' or 'after' sea water tanks from control.

Control was the central station for operational directives and receiving reports. From control, the sub's eye was extended above water, often accompanied by the radio antennas which received, but in times of operational patrol, never transmitted. From control, the ship was steered and depth was controlled. Here, the navigator received information from the two gyro compasses, could take fixes on the stars through the periscope (as a back-up), and charted a course which was electronically indicated in degrees on a digital meter at the steering station.

From here, the officer of the deck (the OD) signaled, by using the bell-order telegraph, a speed change that was acknowledged and responded to by the S.P.C.P. operator in maneuvering. From control, the OD also regulated the submarine's depth and this more than any other one thing determined the submarine's effectiveness and survival. From here, target range, course, and speed were computed and, in the event the order was given, from control the torpedo was fired (after being made ready by the torpedo room watch) and then tracked to target.

All stations were directed or indirectly responsible to control, and it was control that provided the official link that made the submarine a purposeful unit, but not a unique one. The orders and reports were given and received according to precise terminology. The depth and speed changes were directed according to predicable needs and conditions. Somewhere, each submarine had a sister ship, and it too had a control station that functioned the same—it steered the submarine to similar places, for purposes which were also similar in their intent, their intensity, and their secrecy.

Control was the brain and the nervous system, but it was the crew itself that was the heart. And whatever collective life that was uniquely embodied within the thick gray protective shell was in this personality and did not come by directive, and transpired any mechanical or planned purpose.

* * *

(Huffman)

Friends, are you tired of being flailed by your leading petty officers with old rough whips and worn out nutty-knotters? Is your beautiful bod becoming ragged and rough with scar tissue? Well, here's Big Daddy with a money-back for you.

(McGrew)

Oh yeah, cats. Big Daddy's got a real genuine, bonafide deal for you. The Ajax Perversion Whip Company is offering, for a limited time only, the absolute latest in the line of perversion— the company's new model called "The Agony!" Yeah, Baby! This whip is the ideal gift for your L.P.O. on his birthday, at Christmas, on Mother's Day, or any special occasion. Act now cats, because there's a limited supply. Some of the features included in this outstanding offer are your choice of colors (blood red, corpuscle white, or bruise purple) and your favorite kind of material (silk, satin, or synthetic).

After a comprehensive survey of Brooklyn taxis, underground bedrooms, submarines, and other places that pre-verts are known to congregate, it was proved that nine out of ten pre-verts prefer this new model of per-version whip. This whip is guaranteed not, I say not, to leave any welts, scars, or open sores. It will give you only the sheerest, most ultimate experience in horrible pain. Yeah, Baby! Hot Dog! And cats, this whip is going for the unbelievable price of sixty-nine cents while the supply lasts. So, get your cash, check, or money order in to radio S-T-U-D and become one of the happiest pre-verts on board. Oh, Yeah, Baby!

* * *

The training and precision of technique paid off in a smoothness of operation that, in turn, inspired confidence and pride. Phone communication and relaying of orders were exact and always verified by the repetition of the receiver. The very minimum was left to chance as men and systems were interconnected by interlocks to prevent errors, and checks and double checks were made to detect a possible malfunction.

Every critical system, indicator, or procedure had at least one backup or alternative. The steam generator level was monitored by an electric meter, a mechanical meter, and a sight glass. The main engine AC lube oil pumps were backed up by DC pumps, and they, in turn, were backed up by the battery. And all were connected to provide a continuous, no interrupted transition from the primary system to the alternate.

Men too stood ready to quickly take over for each other. Watch stations were manned to allow one to easily overlap into another and during critical times, like battle stations and maneuvering watch, an extra group of men were positioned for the sole purpose of being available for use.

Each man was important. And each crewmember, in his own way, understood the necessity for getting along with everyone else. Every skill was respected, and, underneath the surface, there was very little occupational snobbery. Just as the official atmosphere was smooth, the informal atmosphere was casual and friendly. The crew developed a communication on all levels that was positive and complimentary.

"Join the nuclear navy," the brochure so aptly said, "and become part of a team."

* * *

(DeLay)

Treat me mean and cruel
Treat me like a fool
Ah, yeah, but flail me
You're so cute and smart

Tear my bod apart
C'mon and flail me
Won't ya flail me

Tie me to the EPCP
Do weird things to me
Why don't ya flail me
I won't ask ya to stop
You can be on top,
If you'll just flail me

Chapter XIII

We pulled into the harbor
I heard a man scream
"We're not at a pier
We're tied up in the stream"
Well, I'd rather be keel-hauled
And flailed on a rack
Than to get the bad news that
I'm on back to back
—Radio S.T.U.D.

I

"…listen to me gents, what you say and do will be watched and reflected on all of us as navy men and Americans. Remember, while we're here, every one of us is an ambassador."

Bill nudged Parsons. "Is it true that the last time he was here the X.O. caught the clap?" he whispered.

"No, he has diplomatic immunity," Parsons whispered back.

"…so, if you're asked any questions about the sub or our operations, just say you don't know. And remember these people are mighty sensitive about anything nuclear. As you know, that's why we're going to be in the middle of the harbor instead of moored at the pier. It isn't mine or the engineer's desire to stay steaming (keep the reactor operating), but that's the only way we can do it without shore power. I realize port and starboard liberty and back-to-back watches are far from ideal, but it's better than nothing.

"And, one more thing, make sure you change your money on the base. If you use the black market out in town, those American bucks will ultimately be used against us.

"And if you have a problem...."

"He's going to sing us his theme song," one crewmember whispered to another.

"...but I'm also your friend, so don't hesitate to come and see me. Now, any questions?"

There was a pause for a moment then one of the men shot his hand up.

"Yes, Blanchard?"

"Will you stand by for me tonight?"

[Laughter.]

"That'll be all gents. Blanchard, hold fast, I'd like to see you for a moment."

Bill followed Parsons back to the AMS. Parsons stopped at the workbench and unfolded the schematic that mapped out the circuitry of a PPS (primary protection system) drawer, which lay out on the bench.

"How come no one seemed upset about the fact that they'll be on back to back while we're in Sasabo?" Bill asked.

"They were upset," Parsons said, "But they weren't surprised and that's why they didn't show it."

"But I don't understand why the noseconers are going on port and starboard too. They don't have to be involved in steaming watches."

"Because the old man finally got some smarts, that's why. The sub has one crew, and that crew must work together. There will be plenty for them to be involved in. There are a lot of repairs to be done."

"You seem almost happy about it. How are you going to manage if you spend twenty-four hours on the beach and twenty-four on watch?"

"Best thing that ever happened." Parsons said. "They can't put McGrew and me on twenty-four-hour rotation, and they don't have enough officers to spare two and still get all the liberty they want. So, they're spotting us one officer and qualifying Stewart for R.O.

"Is he ready?"

"No, but he'll learn a lot after he qualifies."

II

Parsons continued to work on the PPS drawer and Bill wandered back to the after end of the AMS. He wasn't due back on watch for another two hours, but he was restless, and he didn't know what to do. They would be in port in about six hours, and he wasn't sure if he was anxious or apprehensive. He felt like a little kid before a big event that was appealing but contained enough of the unknown to also be scary.

Bill sat on the after bench watching a red cloth strip flutter in the breeze from a ventilation blower when his mood was interrupted.

"Hey Carbary."

Bill turned and looked at the lower level AMS watch stander who had popped up halfway through the lower level hatch. Rock Crawford was a big man, but as Bill turned his attention toward him, for some reason, he reminded him of a chipmunk sticking his head up from a hole. Bill noticed that his face looked flushed, and he wondered if he'd been hitting the Gilli again.

"Hey, Carbary, c'mon down here." He disappeared.

Bill proceeded down the ladder and joined Crawford who was sitting on a bench locker in front of the main feed-water station.

"What're ya doing back here now? It's not your watch time." Crawford slapped Bill's knees. "You back here qualifying?"

"Yeah, I was checking out the ventilation system," Bill lied. He noticed that Crawford's eyes looked red.

"Where's your card? Get your qual-card, and I'll check you out on it."

"Well...uh...I'm not quite ready yet."

Crawford jumped up and smacked the lagging on one of the steam pipes with the side of his hand. Dust and small pieces of lagging slowly settled down onto the deck plate and into the bilge.

"Karate," he said. [Whack! Whack!] He hit it twice more and then sat back down.

"What're ya doing back here?" he asked again.

"Qualifying."

"Main steam?"

Bill pulled his qual card from his back pocket. "Ventilation," he said. Crawford picked up a cup from the deck and took a drink. "Have some Gilli,"he offered.

Bill held the cup to his lips and took a small sip. It was one hundred and ninety proof alcohol used for cleaning and had a kick like his father's old ten-gauge. He felt like jumping up and whacking the lagging himself but, instead, he coughed.

Crawford took the card from him and unfolded it. "Who controls the flow of main steam?" he asked.

"The throttle-man," Bill said wiping the water from his eyes.

"Gimmie your pen," Crawford said pulling a pen from Bill's shirt pocket. He scribbled his signature on the card.

Bill looked over to be sure he was signing in the right place. He was surprised that Crawford was being so easy. He had a reputation of being one of the roughest examiners on board. All the non-quals dreaded going to him for ventilation system, but he was the only one authorized to sign it off.

"How about ventilation?" Bill asked, feeling a little hesitant, yet bold enough to not let this opportunity pass.

"You know it?" Crawford asked taking another drink. "Here, have another taste."

Bill took the cup and held it to his lips, but this time he didn't take any. "Well, I know where all the fans are, and I know how the snorkel head valve works and...."

Crawford scribbled again on the card.

Bill took the card from Crawford's hand. As he did, the pen fell from his other hand and bounced off the deck plate into the bilge. Crawford was looking intently at the pipe lagging again. Bill expected him to jump up and whack it at any moment. He was relieved that he had rescued his qual card.

"How come you're drinking now?"

Crawford stared at him.

"Uh...I mean, we'll be in port in a few hours. You're in the liberty section, aren't you?"

Crawford belched. "Yeah, well I thought I'd get a head start. When I hit the beach, I got to find a woman first thing. Don't figure to take the time to get a load on. That's why I'm doing it now. When you're on sea duty, you have got to live fast. That's the way I like it." He jumped up and whacked the lagging again.

The X60J phone circuit rang.

Crawford picked it up. "Lower level AMS, Crawford speaking, sir."

Pause.

"Lower level AMS, aye, Maneuvering."

Crawford laughed. "Sonar called Maneuvering. Said they were picking up a thumping noise that sounded internal to the ship. Thought it might be coming from back here. They want me to check the area to make sure all the gear is stored securely. Crawford got up and started walking forward.

"Where are you going? Bill asked.

"Told ya," Crawford said leaning outboard of number one MG (motor generator). "Got to check for loose gear."

"But—"

"I got the word, and I'm held responsible for doing it. I do my job," Crawford emphasized staring back at Bill. "No one can say I don't."

Crawford walked around the entire lower level checking all storage spaces and then returned to sit by Bill at the feed station. He picked up the X60J phone.

"Maneuvering, Lower level AMS, spaces secure."

Pause.

"Lower Level AMS aye, Maneuvering."

III

The submarine tied up to a barge, which was anchored about two miles out from shore. Every hour, from seven a.m till 10 a.m. and from 3 p.m. till midnight a liberty launch would make a run between the sub and the shore.

It was four-fifty p.m. on the first day when Bill waited on the barge for the launch to arrive. Waiting with him were Parsons, a few other crewmen who had missed the first launch, and a couple of officers. Parsons had stayed to finish the P.P.S. job he had been working on after he had been relieved from the maneuvering watch. Bill wasn't sure if he had volunteered to do this or if he had gotten the word, but he didn't seem bothered about it, so Bill didn't ask.

Parsons hadn't asked Bill to wait for him. He had suggested meeting Bill at the Petty Officer's Club. Bill waited however, and he was rather glad to be separated from the initial surging mass of advancing bodies.

Being in the first section ashore was a mixed bag. Many of the crew jumped at the opportunity, eager to hit the beach as soon as possible. Others were more content to take the first duty and consequently enjoy liberty the last day in Sasabo, which would be Christmas. With Bill, it hadn't mattered. He had felt that Christmas would be, for the most part, just another day—whether he was on liberty or not.

But, as he stood on the barge facing away from the wind with his P-coat collar raised around his cheeks, the memory of past Decembers came back in full force—not because there were many reminders of past Christmases, but more because it was December 20th, and there seemed to be no reminder at all.

He looked back at the bobbing gray cigar-shaped sub, and tried to imagine a Christmas tree somehow implanted in the hull. He gave up this fantasy, however, because it somehow seemed grotesque—for a brief instant, he felt the realization that, analogous to the tree, the submarine itself was a symbol that also got its meaning from the minds of men, but in Bill's mind, the two shared no common mood.

The distant shore was not white with Christmas snow. The water that lay between was not frozen and dotted with ice-skaters, and the air did not carry the echo of ringing Christmas bells. As Bill watched the approaching liberty launch, occasionally puffing the vision out with vapor from his breath, he wondered if the launch would take him away from or closer to his loneliness.

IV

What are they for? Bill thought surveying the most recent bar and feeling that he had been in the same place before. Another beer, another girl—she was a person—she was a person, not just another—no more than he was just another sailor. But, *why*? He looked at Parsons. Parsons would consider it foolish to examine the *why*. But he couldn't help believing—he had to believe that an answer was within him. Was it enough to enjoy or at least pretend to enjoy? and to pass people along the way and never really touch or acknowledge the masks.

Bars. Talk. Drinks. Girls. One girl.

She clung to his arm. She put her head against his shoulder. And she occasionally asked for another drink. He had tried. He had told her about his country and his home. But he could tell that this was not the way. He had been reaching in toward his own feelings and longings but not out. It was part way—halfway maybe, and halfway was better—it must be better—than no way.

He would take her to a hotel and pay her just as she would go with him and take the money. He would say the right things or maybe he wouldn't, but either way the right or wrong words, movements, and actions all counted in a person's favor for total playing time. The only foul was that if he didn't play at all. Bill felt that he could have it either way.

He preferred to be completely open, but he was beginning to understand the threat that this posed for most people. With most people he had come to know, eventually and intermittently the barrier could be broken. It had happened with Janice right away. It had never happened with Barbara, though. With the groups that Bill could remember being a part of, the barrier was never broken—never. He wondered why. It was probably because the game was more intense with a group, and more threatening. But also, in most experiences that he had been part of, it was more entertaining, like a diversion. It was like traveling—going somewhere for sure, but at the same time still enjoying the sights.

He even enjoyed the music—words set to music that described the scenery along the way. Ballads. Traveling. Music. I was dangerous only if he believed that the words rhymed.

He had to keep in mind that the direction of travel was the important thing. And this had to be a direction of his own choosing. When was it that he first recognized his doubt about the structures of what had been laid out for him? He knew that it had been a gradual thing, yet there had been instances that, although he hadn't known it at the time, were to insure a different direction.

Examining his life was like going to confession Bill thought. Going to confession…his thoughts trailed off….

Bill Carbary

* * *

Bill waited in the line behind three other boys in the church. He didn't like to go to confession, but this time the nuns had led the eighth-grade class over directly from the school, so he was stuck. Not that he thought that confession wasn't a good thing. The church had taught him that it was both good and necessary. The fault, of course, was with him. But how could he confess his real feelings?

Surely, no other boy at St. Alphonsus School did such things as he did or had such thoughts. Who else played with themselves, which he knew was bad and intended never to do again, or who, in the whole world would wonder what a nun looked like naked? He hadn't truly confessed yet, and he could not now tell the priest about his true self.

He knew that it would be a mortal sin to deliberately make a bad confession. And equally bad, or perhaps worse, was the mortal sin he committed each time he received communion after having made a bad confession. He knew that, like the many other sinners the nuns so described, his soul must be black with the stain of sin. He vowed to himself that in the future, perhaps next month, he would face up to his sins and make a good confession. He was worried that if he died without doing this, he would surely go to hell. If a person dies with a mortal sin on his soul, he automatically goes to hell. The church had taught him that.

Another boy came out of the confessional, and he moved up one. The boy behind him pinched him on the butt but he said nothing and made no move to indicate that he felt it. He had hardly even noticed it, as he was deep in thought but, even so, he knew that he was in the church, and it was more than the nun's watchful eye that kept him quiet and ever respectful.

He stared blankly at the confessional ahead. It was Father Straub's. More than any other priest, Bill dreaded to go to him. He had a reputation for being gruff and intolerant.

Ironically, he felt protected against drying with sin on his soul. He had made his nine first Fridays and the church (or, at least the nuns at the church of his student-hood) guaranteed that if he went to church nine times in a row on the first Friday of each month, and received communion, then he would not die without first seeing a priest. He wondered, however, if his first Fridays had satisfied the conditions of the guarantee, as he had not made a good confession before going to communion, but he had never heard a priest or a nun qualify the guarantee. He tucked it into his imaginary internal "pocket" and carried it with him on his life's journey.

He wondered if, even in his dying moments, he could confess to the world what he was really like, and the thought struck deep within him that hell, perhaps, was the place he deserved to be. Maybe he was there already.

There was another way though that it might be possible to make things right. He had heard a priest once say that if a person had not gone to confession for a long time, since he probably couldn't remember all his sins, he could make what was called a general confession. All he had to do was say that he had sinned and that he was sorry, and, if he died, he would have to be cleansed in purgatory, but he would be spared the everlasting flames of hell. Bill guessed that he wouldn't mind purgatory so much. At least he wouldn't have to stay there forever. He knew he deserved some punishment.

Another boy left the confessional, and the next boy went in. Now there was only one other boy in front of him, and Bill started to rehearse to himself the lines he would say.

He would not have chosen Father Straub's confessional had he made the choice, but Sister Helen-Marie had divided them up, and it had just been his bad luck. He had experienced Father Straub's famous temper when the father's thunderous disapproval had quickly quieted a rather noisy school breakfast following a first Friday communion. Bill had heard stories about how the father had chased after some boys with a whip. In Bill's eyes, the good father embodied the Lord's *Terrible Swift Sword.*

The boy in the confessional went out and the boy who had been standing in front of Bill went in. It seemed that time was moving very quickly and the confessions of those in front of him seemed to be much briefer than he would have expected. *They probably don't have much to confess,* Bill reasoned, deciding to keep his own confession short. But what if the father could tell that he wasn't telling everything?

No, he would have to have enough sins to convince the father that he was consistent with what he knew must be obvious. He had taken the Lord's name in vain once...no, twice... he had disobeyed his mother about cleaning his room...he had talked in class once when Sister Helen-Marie was out of the room. How long since his last confession? It had been several moths but he couldn't tell the father that. A week? They liked you to go to confession at least once a week. But he didn't deserve to pretend to be that good. Three weeks was more consistent with his intended confession.

The last boy came out and Bill moved into the small box and pulled the heavy purple curtain closed behind him. He knelt on the padded knee rest and leaned toward the small opening covered by a wire screen.

"Bless me, Father, for I have sinned. It has been three weeks since my last confession."

"Three weeks?" came the booming reply, loud enough to be heard all over the church. "Do you think your worldly pleasures are worth making God wait three weeks?"

Bill felt embarrassed, ashamed, and a little angry. "I...uh...I disobeyed."

"Speak up!" Father Straub shouted.

Why doesn't he whisper? Bill thought. *Priests are supposed to whisper.*

Bill continued haltingly on with the father prodding him with what seemed like a pitchfork every time he faltered. Finally, he fumbled through the "sincere act of contrition" and received his penance—fifty "Our Father's" and twenty-five "Hail Mary's"

He left the confessional with his eyes lowered, not wanting to look at the face that he knew must be staring at him. He was embarrassed and angry, and although he didn't consider it at the time, he felt a lot less guilty.

"Hail Mary, full of grace..."

* * *

"What you say, Bill san?" the girl asked looking up at him.

Bill finished the remainder of the beer in the glass he had been holding. "I said it has been nine years since my last confession."

The girl started blankly at him.

Bill looked at the girl and got out his wallet. "And I'm going to commit another sin," he said. "But that's okay, because now I'm eligible for a general."

V

The next morning, the liberty launch was loaded with many tired and hung-over sailors, most of whom had a full day's work and watches to face. Bill sat in the back of the launch next to Parsons who had fallen asleep. Parsons's head bumped on and off Bill's shoulder with each jarring bounce of the boat. Bill remembered the first time he had traveled on a launch out to the Sculpin only a few months before.

It seemed like years instead of months. He knew that he had changed since then, and he wondered if much of this change was determined long ago by the development of group or "crew" attitudes, the original reasons or purposes for which being long since lost, but nonetheless the way to behave being passed on as traditional and therefore sacred. Parallel, but not identical, to this was the 'esprit de corps' sanctioned and legislated by ships' captains and higher ups. It was called morale, and it was judged to be good in that it turned a group into a more dependable reliable unit. Usually independent of both these things was the purpose of the mission and, unless this mission itself was fanciful, it was generally kept apart from the perpetual fantasies which were fed by laughter, not logic.

Bill nudged Parsons.

"Huh?" Parsons opened his eyes.

"I'm glad I ripped off a piece last night," Bill said grinning.

"You woke me up to tell me that? What're ya talking about?"

"Well, tomorrow we might die."

"Yeah, war's hell," Parsons said closing his eyes again.

VI

Bill and Parsons had the first EPCP and RPCP watch. There were only three watch standers in maneuvering including the EOOW, as the throttle man station (SPSP) didn't need to be manned.

"Hey, Mr. Browder," Parsons said. I saw you at the Black Rose last night. How much did you have to pay for that snapper I saw you with?"

"Are you referring to my date for the evening?"

Parsons laughed. "Naw, I didn't see Mr. Welty there. I'm talking about that lady of the night. You know, the one with the ratty hair and the front teeth missing. How much yen did she cost you? Did she give you a nobber or did you just have her kiss your ass?" He turned to Bill. "Did you know that officers have candy asses?"

Bill didn't answer. He wondered if Parsons had finally gone too far.

"Alright, that's enough, Parsons," Browder said, "turn around and face your panel."

"What time you going over tomorrow?" Parsons asked Bill.

"Don't know. Might be nice to get some sleep before I hit the beach."

"You'd be smart not to sleep on here during your liberty time. If you are easily accessible, you are considered available, and if they need you, they'll snap you up."

"You're getting even less sleep than most of us," Bill said. "What are you going to do?"

"I'm going to get a hotel room after I go to the exchange and have a good meal at the Petty Officer's Club."

"I want to hit the exchange also. I need to send home some stuff for Christmas. Mind if I come along?"

"Sure. You want to come too, Mr. Browder?"

"No thanks Parsons. I…uh…figure to be busy tomorrow."

Parsons laughed.

VII

"This is the life," Parsons said sipping some wine.

Bill put his fork down. "Isn't that a little out of character for you? Usually you're complaining about the shit you claim keeps getting dumped all over you."

"Well, it's true you know. They try to do me, but anyway, I can handle that. I believe that when a man has liberty in a foreign port or anywhere for that matter, that he is in control, and the seas may be rough or calm, but it's great to have the helm."

"You got water on the brain," Bill said.

Parsons took out a long thin cigar, unwrapped it, put it in his mouth, and lit it. "Look around Bill, could you think of a better place to be right at this moment?"

"Might be nice to be home for Christmas," Bill said honestly.

Parsons blew smoke. "Yeah, and doing the same things you always have. I'll bet that all your Christmases are the same." Parsons took another puff on the cigar and then butted it in his coffee cup. "I think the real exciting joy of life is having new experiences and being the master of them."

Bill took a drink of his coffee. "I dunno," he said grinning. "I can think of some old experiences I wouldn't mind reliving."

A waitress came to the table and started picking up some of the dishes. "You want anything else?" she asked, reaching for and then changing her mind about picking up the coffee cup with Parsons's cigar sticking out.

"I'd like some more coffee," Bill said.

Parsons poured some more wine into his glass as the waitress left. "You ought to try some of this," he said. "Life is full of experiences that people don't know they'll like until they try them."

"That may be true," Bill said, "but it's also full of a lot of experiences that draw on a man's strength. I think a person has to discriminate—you can't do and try everything, and you can't be everything."

"That's pretty heavy," Parsons said.

"I don't know about your bit about living for new experiences. It's not that I don't necessarily believe in it. I just don't think you really do."

The waitress returned and poured Bill a fresh cup of coffee.

"I mean you bitch and moan about your life in the navy, but you really love it."

"Well, I told you I did," Parsons said. He took a drink of wine. "I don't love being had, though. I like meeting new people and going to new places. I like doing a job that is not predictable."

Bill put sugar and cream in his coffee and stirred it. "The places, the job, and even the people might be new, but still I think a lot of people in their actions and re-actions make it pretty much all the same."

"Whaddaya mean?"

"Well, you know Crawford?"

"Yeah."

"How long's he been in?"

"Fourteen years I think give or take one or two. Why, whaddaya talking about? Rock's a good head."

"He is. But he's all one-sided."

"Hey, hold on," Parsons said. Nobody knows his job better than Rock. And, if you ever get in trouble on the beach, I can't think of anyone I'd rather have on hand than Rock. He's a good ol' boy."

Bill spooned his coffee. "I like Rock," he said. "Don't get me wrong. It's just that I think there's more to life than being what you call a good ol' boy. I think a man has to grow and change, and I see too many people in the navy who just don't do it."

Parsons held his glass up until the wine was gone. "Well, a person could be a lot worse off than to be like Rock," he said. Besides, you can't blame the navy. Look at those executives in those big city companies if you want to see people who never change and lead a dead life besides.

"Yeah, I know what you mean," Bill said. "I guess I just don't want to end up whacking the lagging."

"Huh?"

Bill picked up his white hat. "C'mon let's pay our check and get out of here. How about if we go get drunk and laid."

"Sounds reasonable," Parsons said standing up. "And maybe, if we're lucky, we can kick ass on a couple of skimmer shore patrol."

Chapter XIV

Three days of duty and three on the town
My brain is confused and my body's run down
But who gives a damn, a hoot, or a hell
We'll have sixty days to make ourselves well

—Radio Station S.T.U.D.

I

"There's no turning back now gents, we'll be on patrol the day after tomorrow."

Bill only caught patches of the X.O.'s comments. If he craned his neck, he could see the map on the bulkhead of the crew's mess, but he didn't bother.

"At no time will we go within twelve miles of shore. Nothing that we will do will be illegal by international law...."

Bill figured he could be fully qualified back aft in another two weeks and then he should be able to finish his qualification on the whole boat by the end of the second patrol. He'd love to have dolphins by the time the sub returned to San Diego, and he took leave for home.

"...where we go and what we do is strictly confidential...."

He wondered when another S.T.U.D. tape would be played. He enjoyed the tapes and, like almost the entire crew, he looked forward to the next one. Time, in this world, could be measured as periods between two S.T.U.D. tapes he decided. The D.J. bit was laughter. The songs often played in his mind and occupied his thoughts with a fantasy invited and welcome.

We are the men from that steaming SSN
There is not a port that got a girl we will miss
We've spread our fame throughout the land
From Mexico unto Japan
Look out Pearl because you're next on our list.

Pearl Harbor. Supposed to stop there on the way back Bill thought.

"...communications technicians will be hot-bunking with you gents. It'll be inconvenient but unavoidable, so make them feel welcome...."

'Spooks,' Bill thought. Not C.T.s but 'spooks.' That's what the crew called them—the men who were not officially on board. They were deliberately left off the sailing list so as not to give away the type of mission the sub would be on.

"They are welcome any time in my rack," Niles said stroking a nearby spook on the head.

The X.O. glared at him.

"That's all men," the X.O. said as Bill contemplated raising his hand and asking him to review again the cover story to be told in the event of capture, but then thought better of it.

Oh hell, Bill thought, I'd just say that I was swimming in the ocean off the coast of San Diego when I was swallowed by this metal whale. The ridiculousness of this amused him, and he decided to relay this fantasy to McGrew or DeLay for possible incorporation into a S.T.U.D. tape.

We all live in a little metal whale
A little metal whale, a little metal whale

Bill Carbary

We all live in a little metal whale
A little metal whale, with a little metal sail

All my friends they are pre-verts
And the chow, it really hurts
Oh, we never get no mail
When we live in a metal whale

We all live in a little metal whale
A little metal whale, A little metal whale
We all live in a little metal whale
A little metal whale, with a little metal sail

Here we are, we are out at sea
No pretty women, no liberty
Oh, what I'd give for a little tail
And to get off this metal whale

We all live…

Metal whales are not too neat
All you do is sleep and eat
Might as well be in a jail
As to live in a metal whale

We all live…

—Radio Station S.T.U.D.

II

Bill had experienced what he thought was a continuous repetitive routine, but it had been nothing like being on patrol. Almost everything was slowed down to reduce the overall noise of the submarine. Often two entire watch periods would go by without a bell change, as the sub creeped along at one-third. The only change seemed to be the state of the sea when the submarine eased up to a shallow depth to eject garbage, blow sanitaries, and peak through the scope. At these times, when the sea was restless enough to unpredictably jostle this portable world, it seemed to Bill to be a welcome reminder—a reminder that, in fact, there was an external world *out there.*

Like the mechanical world around them, the men too seemed to have shifted into a slow-motion mode of movement. Almost everyone resigned themselves to the two-month mutual isolation and knew from either experience, insight, or instinct that a casual surrender to routine, procedure, and easy relationships eased them toward the next watch, the next day, and the next liberty port in a tolerable manner. There was always one or more that didn't adjust, however, and time, like the bulkheads of the submarine, closed in on them. Donald Cook was such a man.

Cook was a small red-haired person who had quit high school at sixteen and joined the navy, with his father's permission, immediately upon his seventeenth birthday. He had been in the navy barely a year when he came aboard the submarine as a sonar man striker. He was not prepared for, nor did he understand, the inevitable indoctrination and regarded the practical jokes and put-ons as threatening verifications that he was indeed picked on and not well liked.

"Cookie," as he had first been called, reminded Bill of a boy that he had known in high school—a person who had struck out in rage and frustration at being at the bottom of the pecking order, often misread intentions and situations as personal attacks, and continually entrenched his social position. He engaged in inconsistent and miss-directed efforts to change what he inwardly believed was inevitable. Others usually react to such people by ignoring or tormenting them, and this seems to all concerned as the natural order of things.

On the Sculpin, however, Cookie or "Crumb," as he was soon to be called, was not ignored and the crewmembers who accommodated his expectations were performing the duties of submariners. On one occasion, Cook had tried to fight, after receiving a friendly "Thanksgiving goose." This confirmed in most minds the unreliability of the new man's reactions. Once Cook had been thus classified, all further foul-ups were welcomed with knowing expectations and open insinuations that someone had fucked up by sending him to the sub in the first place. It was generally accepted, without being generally verbalized, that it was each man's responsibility to help see to it that "Crumb" was shipped out as soon as possible.

III

Bill was relieved early from the twelve to four afternoon EPCP watch and headed up to the crew's mess. It was especially advantageous to get relieved early from the twelve to four's because this enabled a man to find a good seat in the crew's mess for the movie, which would start following soup call.

As he slid into one of the table benches facing the movie screen, the crew's mess began to empty of many of the relieving watch standers. Bill was sipping on his first bowl of soup when other relieved watch standers began filtering in. He figured to go slow on his soup and sandwich so as not to be accused of camping in a good movie seat and causing others to eat soup call standing up. Of course, this was a common practice, but the ones who were most famous for it would be the loudest if someone could be caught hogging a seat without actually eating.

Before all the seats on the bench where Bill was sitting became filled, though, Cook came down from standing a trainee watch in Control and squeezed in opposite Bill. Bill took notice of this, but he didn't say anything and continued to go through the process of not eating. He realized after a moment though that Walt Hazard, the man sitting next to Bill, had been staring at Cook since he had sat down. He could tell that Cook was aware of it also because, although he didn't look up, his obvious decision not to look up indicated his uneasiness. Hazard was determined, however, and, after several minutes of stoic staring, he locked Cook in after the glance he had been waiting for.

"You stink," Hazard said picking up his soup and moving away from the table.

The other men at the table, who by this time had become aware of Hazard's game, without hesitation did the same. Only Bill and Cook remained.

Bill had not been surprised at what had happened, out he had not allowed himself to anticipate the situation. Even in remaining, he had not internalized his decisions or even surfaced thoughts that a decision had been made—he was there to eat soup and wait for a movie, no more.

"Why can't they leave me alone?" Cook asked.

I'm not your friend; Bill's thoughts shouted loud enough it seemed for everyone to hear.

"Do you think I stink?"

For the first time since the other men left, Bill looked up from his soup bowl. *Why is he questioning me?* he thought. I'm a qualified watch stander and a petty officer—he's just a...a... striker. Bill thought for a brief instant about Captain Vogel.

"Uh...that's not what he meant," Bill said.

Cook slammed his fist down on the table.

"I know what he meant," he shouted. "What they all mean. What they have *always* meant."

Bill knew without looking that those who had not been staring before now were, but he also realized that it really didn't bother him as much as he would have thought it would.

"They mean to push you as far as you'll let them," Bill said looking Cook in the eye for the first time.

"I've heard that before," Cook said. "But why should I fight back for...for...," Cook motioned with his head and his hand around himself, "this?"

"Fight back for yourself," Bill said.

"No, you mean fight back to lose myself—to become a phony like all the rest of you so I won't embarrass you anymore."

"The crew has to depend on each other for—"

"For what? For helping each other pretend to be big men? You guys ought to start a religion."

Bill thought for a moment of the Catholic religious instruction classes he had to take when he went to public high school. Funny, he could remember well going to the classes, but he couldn't remember anything that took place in the classes. He wondered how long he had been resisting organized religion.

Bill looked back at Cook. "What are you going to do?" he asked.

Cook stood up and started moving away. He left his soup bowl on the table, breaking the rule. "What are *you* going to do?" Cook said, or at least Bill thought he said that.

Hazard pushed Cook when he got out in the aisle. "What's a matter Crumb, you too good to clean up after yourself?"

Another crew member received Hazard's pass and Cook was physically transferred down the passageway by the standing men.

"Shove him in that shit can," Hazard called out.

Bill heard the clank of the can cover. He wondered why he didn't hear Cook's protests and, at the same time, he wondered why he didn't hear any of his own.

"Hey, when's the movie going to start?" Part of the crew called out in a voice which, to Bill, sounded like it could have been his own.

IV

Bill watched half of the movie even though he had decided after the first five minutes that he didn't like it. Finally, he squeezed out of the crew's mess and went down to his bunk. He wasn't tired, and he tried to read but each word seemed isolated and he wasn't getting into it. Giving up on reading, he shut his bunk light off, closed his eyes, and slowly moved into a dream that started before he was completely asleep.

* * *

He was alone on a submarine where everything was automatic. Pumps ran and shut off, valves opened and closed, and even the battery charge was an automatic function of the machine that carried him to... to... he didn't know. He would sleep, eat, and walk around the submarine for four hours— always being in the same place at the same time. His food was always waiting at the same time, and it was always the same—chipped beef on toast. It seemed natural to think that he would automatically know what to do if something needed to be done, but he also came to expect that he would continue to experience things as he had come to expect they would be.

The only thing that he physically acted upon was a small red button that he pressed. This button was located on the bulkhead next to a small door near his bunk. It was the last thing he did before going to sleep. For some reason, he assumed that the button released drops of oil on a machine that was behind the door, but he never looked.

Finally, a day came and something happened that was different from before—the submarine stopped. Somehow, he knew that it was not something that had gone wrong but that a destination had been reached, and he found himself standing in front of the small door. Through his dream, he saw himself automatically open the door and remove a reel of tape from some type of machine inside. He took a new tape from a bottom compartment and placed it on the machine where the previous tape had been. Then he pressed the red button. He could see, as the door slowly closed, that the machine was re-winding the new tape.

* * *

He woke up with a cold sweat on his forehead, and he partially sat up in his bunk with his elbows propped beneath him. From the ship's entertainment speaker, he could hear music and lyrics and he listened intently to pick out the meaning of the words.

Oh, it's hard, ain't it hard, ain't it hard
To leave your love and then go out to sea
Oh, it's hard, ain't it hard, ain't it hard
Great God!
To stay out here and never to be free
For the past thirty days, we've been steaming
Beneath the waves is where we always go
Now my sex glands sure are screaming
And my dungarees are starting to get holes

Oh, it's hard, ain't it hard, ain't it…

It's not hard, Bill thought, rolling out of his bunk onto the floor. It's not hard enough.

V

Bill was bothered by some of the crew attitudes and the consequential burden this placed on him in the form of unspoken expectations. The incident with Cook made him wonder at the value of a system that seemed to function on a large scale by total acceptance or total rejection. He partially interpreted his dream as a warning that he should guard against becoming just a mechanical piece of a larger unthinking unit. But still he understood the value of passing time easily and casually and not dwelling on things that he had little power to change. He felt, in time, a deeper understanding and perhaps even a decision would come to him, but for now the submarine and its luring atmosphere still provided an absorbing attraction. He did decide to avoid accepting it blindly or surrendering to it totally; however, he would reserve part of himself to be himself and this he knew was very important.

VI

The AEF (Auxiliary Electrician Forward) was one of the two remaining watch stations Bill had yet to qualify on. The other station was the shutdown maneuvering area watch (SMAW) and, once this requirement was completed, Bill would be finished with the nuclear part of the submarine qualification.

Standing training watches for AEF meant that Bill would have to spend all his watch time in the forward spaces, and for this reason, he had put off this qualification for as long as he could. There were two other forward watch stations that he had already qualified on, but they were stationary watch stations under the direct control of the DOD. The AEF, however, like the AEA was a roving watch stander and this made him convenient for use as a fetch and return person and, also, a practical joke tester for stationary conspirators.

The AEF was in many ways, however, a much better watch to stand than the AEA. There was nowhere near the number of readings to take, the noise of the engine room was refreshingly absent, and food and coffee were handy. The nuclear trainees on the AEF watch were always sure to receive an extra hard time, however, and Bill knew he would be no exception.

Bill stood the twelve to four's. He was glad to get that watch section, because if he had gotten the four to eight's, he would have had to wake up non-quals to work on their daily qualifications. He didn't mind waking the regulars for their periodic watches but rousting the men who were in a lower caste system and therefore got less sleep bothered him.

The spooks seemed to take care of their own schedules. They always seemed to be where they were supposed to be and seldom were anywhere where they appeared obvious. Bill knew that their label was a joke, but like some people who seemed to look like their names, the spooks seemed to behave like theirs. It was therefore rather surprising when one of the spooks approached Bill and asked him to help him out on learning the forward electrical system. Bill's first reaction was to be suspicious that he was being set up, but the man finally convinced him that he really wanted to qualify on the submarine. The man's name was Sam Olson.

Bill didn't know everything about the forward electrical layout, but he was able to figure out what he didn't know by reading fuse boxes and cable tags. It took more than an hour, but Bill did not begrudge the time or the activity—he knew that by showing and explaining it would help him understand and remember better. And Sam was methodical—he took notes as he went along, and he insisted upon crawling in or behind wherever he would fit to see that which was not obvious. Bill himself had been that motivated at first but his philosophy as of late had been to do and learn only as much as necessary to get by. It made him uneasy, but also curious to see someone so intent on doing more without the threat of learn or burn.

Bill sipped coffee and looked across at Sam who was still making notes.

"Will you be able to wear them if you get them?" Bill asked.

"Oh yeah," Sam said. "I just won't be able to say where or when I qualified."

"It's a lot of work to do in two months. You got anything signed off yet?"

"Just main and vital hydraulics."

"That's a big one," Bill said. "Is it worth losing sleep over? You might not make it you know."

"You mean I probably won't make it. You're not the first person who has pointed that out. I think I will. But, regardless, I'll go as far as I can, and if I don't have time to finish, what I will have done will be enough."

"Enough for what?" Bill put more sugar in his coffee and then looked at his watch. He would have to take readings soon.

"Enough for the time I spent," Sam said. "I don't look on things as all or nothing or as being isolated. Sure, I'd like a set of dolphins to wear on my chest but even if I don't finish, what I have done will be a piece of who I am."

"I appreciate what you're saying," Bill said. I've had similar feelings myself. But lately I've been wondering just how much control we really have over our...our...," Bill shrugged.

"Our destiny?" Sam asked. "I don't know about that. One thing I don't worry about though is the sleep I lose because I'm *doing* something. I feel that the dreams that come from too much sleep are uncontrolled pieces of us that are unraveling."

VII

Bill stood the AEF training watch for a week during which time he received only minor hassling and a few half-hearted attempts at put-ons that really didn't catch him off guard. He did get some static about not getting Dingle up every night at the usual relieving time. Dingle stood the torpedo room watch, and he was notorious for being a late reliever. Bill knew that he was not really blamed for Dingle's continual lateness, as it was common knowledge that it took almost a stick of dynamite to get Dingle out of his bunk.

Bill was therefore curious when he caught part of a conversation about a plan that would be sure to cure Dingle's problem—"either that or eliminate him," he heard someone say, accompanied by a chorus of laughter.

From the reputations of the individuals engaged in this plan, Bill knew that it had to be a joke of some sort. He tried to find out what was going to happen but all they would tell him was that it was set up for the 3:45 relief and that he would be there when it happened. They insisted that Bill wait until they were relieved from their watches before he started to wake Dingle up the first time. This was unusual, but it didn't seem to be objectionable, as the person Dingle was supposed to be relieving was getting a special relief, so he would be in on it also. Bill was a little concerned that they might be setting him up, but he didn't figure he was a big enough fish to warrant the scope of the plan that he sensed was in the offering.

There were five men standing alongside of Bill in the passageway when he shook Dingle the first time. Dingle just turned over, and he didn't even grunt until Bill shook him again.

"Okay, he's had his chance," one of the men said.

Another man laughed.

"Hey! What's all this noise for?" a man in an adjacent bunk said.

"Shhhhhh"

"Put the tape on"

Bill looked on while one of the men started covering the opening to Dingle's bunk compartment with high-pressure tape.

"What're ya doing that for?" Bill asked.

"So, he won't get out," someone said.

"Don't we want him out?" Bill asked.

"Shhhhhh," a voice admonished.

"Okay, that's enough tape, let's pull the cord."Gumit reached under Dingle's mattress and stood ready for the command.

"Whaddaya got under there?" Bill asked.

"An inflatable life raft," someone whispered.

"You guys crazy? You're going to crush him!"

"Naw. It's not a twelve-man, only a four-man."

"Ya want me to pull?"

"Wait one," Hazard said. "Let's put the fear of God in him." Hazard reached through the crisscross tape and poked Dingle. "Dingle, get up or the giant pussy of fate will envelope your whole body!"

"Goddamnit! Leave me alone. Let me sleep," Dingle grunted.

"Pull!"

Whooosh—shhhhhh....

"Aughhhhhhhh."

Dingle's arm shot out through an opening in the tape, flailed around for a moment, and then it was motionless. Dingle's strangled scream was loud at first, then muffled, and finally silent.

"Ya think he's awake?" Gumit asked.

"Hey, Dingle, you awake?"

[Laughter.]

"You sure he's not dead?" Bill asked, and at the same time, wondered why he was not doing something to help him.

"Jesus, maybe we'd better pull him out," Hazard said as he grabbed Dingle's arm. Two others joined the pull and Dingle popped out pulling the tape with him.

Granny listened for a heartbeat on the chest of the still motionless body while someone grabbed a battle lantern and shined it on his face.

"He's still alive," Granny said.

"Goddamnit! Leave me alone. Let me sleep," Dingle said, shielding his face from the light with his arm, as he turned over on his side and went back to sleep.

Chapter XV

I wonder why I celebrate
My yesterdays are all gone
And the dreams I have for tomorrow
Seems somehow to be wrong
But today is here, I hold it near
And feel its moving beat
And I can't describe the pull inside
To advance or to retreat
So, swept along I join the throng
And I truly do rejoice
To be relieved, to be deceived
By the party of my choice

—Bill

I

The steady vibration of the submarine at full speed was a welcome change after two months of routine sameness. But more than that, it was a tangible signal that the patrol had ended and that, at last, a destination was being sought—being sought with deliberate incautious determination. Yokosuka, Japan. An eleven-day stop-over before the next patrol. Eleven days could be forever. Thought of as a total block of time, it didn't seem very long. But as disjointed moments, as an accumulation of unique experiences, as anticipated expectations, and finally as embellished memories—it could be forever.

Many of the crew had been to Yokosuka before. Certainly, everyone had experienced Sasabo. But the patrol had changed things, not in the external world that lay ahead, but in the personalities of the men who were to be there. These personalities were, in varying degrees, different now from before. Bill knew this, and he felt that the other men knew it as well. He had only been on one patrol—yet he knew that each one would have a unique effect on a group personality, and consequently on the individual.

And this seemed totally and, reasonably so, completely apart from the external mission. Bill sensed that this was not an isolated occurrence, but one common to many kinds of group undertakings. And he wondered if this factor might be more significant than all the preconceived purposes and the objectively evaluated results.

And what did his yesterdays have to do with this? And where and what would his tomorrows be because of it? He didn't know. He was only certain that the experiences of "today" were more important now than they ever had been before.

Because such experiences of the moment were of intense importance, they were sought after with an unacknowledged exactitude. Seemingly random choices of time and presence would unite personalities together in frantic and near bursting exhilaration. Some appeared coincidental; some were planned gatherings. And the results ranged from drunken brawls to concerted carnal depravity.

As the personified portable world obediently moved across time and narrowed a distance, its inhabitants, like moths approaching a flame, fervently planned a group celebration, as the intensity of their anticipation grew greater.

Bill had never been to a ship's party before, but he had heard all the stories. He was most amused by the tale of Abe Johnson, a supposedly mild-mannered Sonarman who drank too much at one of the parties and disappeared about three a.m. howling into the night. He wasn't seen again until seven o'clock that same morning when he came hot-footing across the sub pier parking lot completely naked. Luckily, one of the sub's officers was just coming back to the boat, and he managed to get Johnson across the sub tender quarterdeck with a minimum of hassle.

Apparently, Johnson didn't remember what had happened or at least he said he didn't. Anyway, Johnson had been transferred shortly after that incident. Parsons claimed that the X.O. undoubtedly instigated the transfer. He said that the X.O. couldn't stand to see anyone having a good time.

The transfer notwithstanding, Bill got the impression the wild behavior of a ship's party was expected, encouraged, and then immortalized until surpassed by the next incident. The San Diego parties with many wives present, and without the overwhelming excuse to drown the memories of a two-month patrol, surely would have to be considered "tame" when compared to the coming event.

It was scheduled for the first Thursday evening in port. The banquet room of the Enlisted Men's Club was available that evening and confirmation had been made by radio.

The sub was due in on a Tuesday, and the anticipated duty section for the coming Thursday evening was pared down to just the minimum necessary. Bill would be off, but Parsons had gotten stuck with the duty. Stewart was being transferred as soon as the sub reached port, and this meant there would only be two qualified R.O.s again, and with only two, the party-night duty man had been decided by the flip of a coin— Parsons lost.

This time the sub would be tied up to a pier and be on shore power, which made everyone happy except Parsons. He figured that if the submarine were to stay steaming again, they would have to keep Stewart at least through this liberty period to help man the R.O. steaming watch. With the reactor shut down, though, he would still be on port and starboard, as an R.O. had to be on board any time the sub was in the water, and the rest of the crew would be on three-section liberty.

Parsons vowed to get drunk the night of the party anyway, and Bill didn't doubt that he would. As for the rest of the crew, Bill noticed that, for the most part, the usual after watch drinking had stopped on the way toward port. Bill reasoned that this was due to a more relaxed atmosphere, as the patrol had ended, or perhaps there was some desire to simulate the sixty-one days "dry" that would provide a purported reason for getting drunk on party night or, more likely, the booze supply had been exhausted.

Bill's thoughts about the party were mixed. Certainly, he was a piece of the group personality and, as such, he received and gave encouragement to the growing expectations. But of no less significance, he was an individual, and it was this individual self that had been magnified by introspection in the previous few months, and this inner self seemed to be pulling in a different direction from the part of him that was part of the group.

Strangely, Parsons acted as a bellows which, at different times, fanned the flames of both parts of Bill. He was not Bill's only friend, but when Bill thought of being without him at the party, he had a feeling that he would be very much alone. Perhaps not really alone—he guessed that he would really be, for the most part, uninfluenced, and this was an even more disturbing realization than the anticipation of loneliness—for Bill sensed that he might have to make a choice, and although he felt he would be ready to do this, he was not yet ready to want to.

II

The music from the band was quite loud. They were a Japanese group that imitated the American rock sound with a mixture of American and Japanese lyrics. They provided an absorbing pulsating beat that was both as close to and at the same time as separated from true American music as the sailors and girls were from each other.

Bill was usually bothered by loud music, but now it seemed appropriate. It made conversation impractical and shielded him from interruptions that would require an expected response on his part. For now, the input was all one way, and for now, that was the only way that Bill wanted it.

Most of the crew had arrived with their girls. Most had planned a day or two in advance with a particular girl. Bill had not. It hadn't been that important. It wasn't that he didn't want one for the party; it was just too easy a thing to worry about. He'd get a girl later; all he needed was money, and he had that. Either that or he'd borrow someone else's girl—what the hell, what difference did it make?

He would just let it happen, he couldn't chase and grab for it—he wouldn't—he had to take things as they came, and then the results wouldn't matter. He wouldn't make their mistake. But he was part of them. Was that the choice? Or was he just drunk? He looked at his glass and swirled the ice cube around in the bourbon. He hadn't drunk that much. Besides, it was too early to be drunk. He made up his mind. He wouldn't be drunk yet.

"Hi Bill."

Bill turned and looked at Gabby who had his arm draped around the neck of a pretty girl in a red satin-like dress. Bill smiled. They all have red satin-like dresses, he thought.

"Whaddaya think of her?" Gabby shouted above the music. "Nice, huh?"

"Uh…yeah," Bill said.

"Don't worry, she can't understand any English. Isn't that neat? I found one that ya don't have to carry on a conversation with."

"They're rare, alright," Bill grinned. "How do you et her know what you want?"

"You kidding? They all understand what 'fuck' means."

The girl looked up at Gabby, and he laughed. "See what I mean? Here, you watch her while I go fill up my glass." Gabby squeezed the girl's right breast. "You stay here. Honey, I'll be right back." He turned to Bill. "Neat, huh? That's how I tell her to stay."

"What happens if you squeeze her left breast?" Bill called after Gabby, but his question was lost to all except the girl who caught his gaze, as he turned back.

"I'll suck your cock till your head caves in," the girl said in perfect English.

"Oh, Jesus," Bill said as he met the girl's stoic stare and then stood transfixed for what seemed like minutes unable to think of what to say next. "Ya wanna dance?" he finally said as the band started another number.

III

"I jess wanna let you men know...."

The Captain stood on the raised stage with both hands clasping the standing microphone. The head table, right in front of the stage, was manned by the officers and their dates. The captain's chair, now empty, faced away from the stage toward the dance floor. Next to the empty chair, the captain's date sat turned toward the stage with her right arm sticking up the Captain's left pant leg all the way to the elbow.

No one seemed to be listening to the captain. The various conversations continued, and on the dance floor, a sai or and his date, wrapped in each other's arms, swayed back and forth without moving their feet, and on the opposite end of the floor, two sailors did the jitterbug.

The band had taken a break, but it was as if no one noticed for new events had their own momentum.

"…as fine a crew as ever served on any sub…."

Dingle had his arm over the shoulder of one of the new crew members who had met the sub in Yokosuka. "It takes getting used to," Dingle said. "It even took me awhile, but if you've got what it takes, then it'll seem funny when you're on dry land. Shit, after that last patrol, it took a whole day before it felt natural to walk on a flat deck that didn't move."

"How are you doing now, Dingle?" Garcia said, entering the conversation.

Dingle laughed and then downed his remaining half glass of booze. "Running hot, straight, and normal," he said.

"I'd stay away from him if I were you," Garcia said to the new man. "He thinks he's a torpedo."

Some of the men had already left the party with their girls to find a hotel. Others with the same idea, and more imagination, were using the adjoining coatroom, closets, and hallways. A couple of the more adventurous had even tried the kitchen, but the club manager had run them out. Bill figured it would be only a matter of time until the corners and wall booths would be filled with copulating bodies.

Bill caught pieces of conversation from different groups, as he wandered drink in hand, but not drinking. It seemed that he was a separated observer, and what he saw encompassed more than just that which was immediately before him. He remembered, and he listened, and he momentarily lost the sense of identifying with anything other than the blend of his transformation in getting here and the experience of being here.

"The Cob wants us to move him from the dance floor."

"What for? Ain't sleepwalking. Shit, he ain't walking at all."

"C'mon let's move him before he barfs all over the floor. You get his feet."

"…come a long way, but we still have a way to go before we return to our loved ones…."

"I wonder what his 'loved one' would say if she knew some slant eye had her arm up his pant leg?"

Over in the corner, Bill noticed the naked legs of a girl jerking rhythmically.

The Captain had passed out with his head down on the table and the club manager, seemingly undaunted by the captain's condition, stood above him with his arms flailing and his jaws flapping.

"We are the men from that steaming SSN...."

Bill heard a tape playing. Or, was the 'tape' in his head? It was a fleeting thought and quickly forgotten.

"...there's not a port that's got a girl we'll miss, we've spread our fame throughout the land from Mexico unto Japan"

The two wide double doors, which led into the room, burst open and five shore patrol issued in upholstering their clubs as they entered.

"...and I'm sure when we depart we will take a thousand hearts and leave a page in your perversion history...."

One of the shore patrol blew his whistle, and as if on signal, the captain jumped to his feet.

"Dive! Dive! Dive!" he shouted as a bottle rolled across his table and crashed on the floor below.

IV

Bill stared out of the third-floor window toward the harbor. The sun was just rising, and it was light enough to make out part of the waterfront. Somewhere out there a submarine waited. He looked at his watch. It was 6:12 now. By nine, he would have to be back on board. He sighed. Back to the real world, he thought, and then the awareness of this thought made him smile. He realized that somewhere between last night and this morning he had turned a corner, and he no longer regarded the "submarine life" as a threat or a temptation. And neither was it just a stopover on the way to something more permanent. He understood that he would not always be a submarine sailor, and he was grateful that he would not have to someday realize that he had never been a submarine sailor.

He had an instantaneous urge to open the window and shout, "Fuck you Frank!" as he sailed his white hat down to the street below. He resisted. *Life must have some restraints,* he thought. He turned and walked toward the bed. "But just a few," he said out loud, as he reached down and squeezed the left breast of the girl in the bed.

She opened her eyes and smiled.

***

A group, a hoard, of beggars stored
So neatly in a stall
And piece by piece, a dragon's feast
Of knights within a hall
And queens and kings and stately things
All gathered for a ball
Within, without, they scream, they shout
And clamor till they fall
And down below, an imagined foe
Gives out a fearsome call
And soon they'll be, but they'll never see
Underneath it all

—Bill (with a little help from Liam)

Not quite The End

(Please read the epilogue)

Epilogue

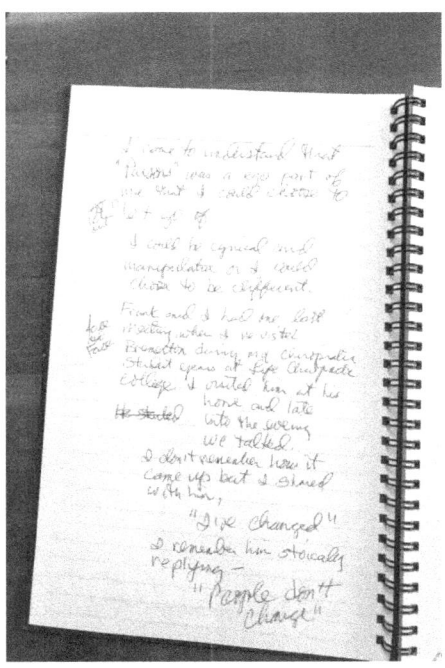

I came to understand that "Parsons" was an ego part of me that I could choose to let out, or let go of.

I could be cynical and manipulative, or I could choose to be different.

Frank and I had one last face-to-face meeting when I re-visited Bremerton during my chiropractic student years at Life Chiropractic College (West).

I visited him at his home and, late into the evening, we talked. I don't remember how it came up, but I shared with him.

"I've changed."

I remember him stoically replying: "People don't change."

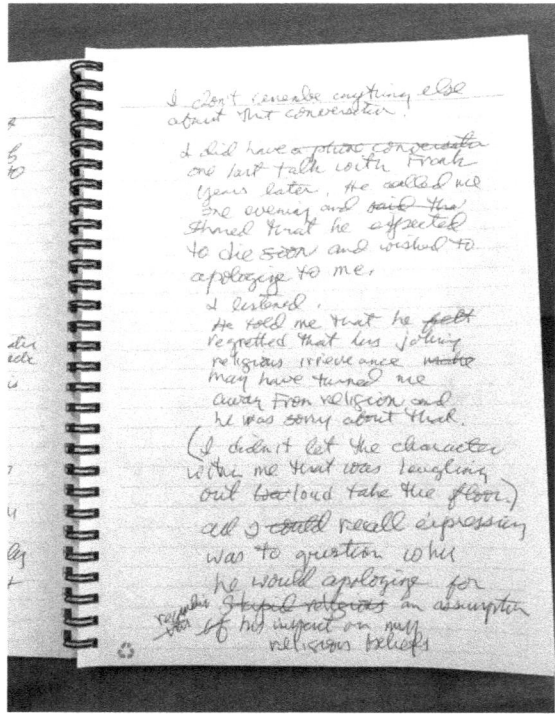

I don't remember anything else about that conversation.

I did have one last talk with Frank years later. He called me one evening and shared that he expected to die soon and wanted to apologize to me.

I listened. He told me that he regretted that his joking religious irreverence may have turned me away from religion, and he was sorry about that.

(I didn't let the character within me that was laughing out loud take the floor.)

All I recall expressing was to question why he would apologize for an assumption regarding his impact on my religious beliefs.

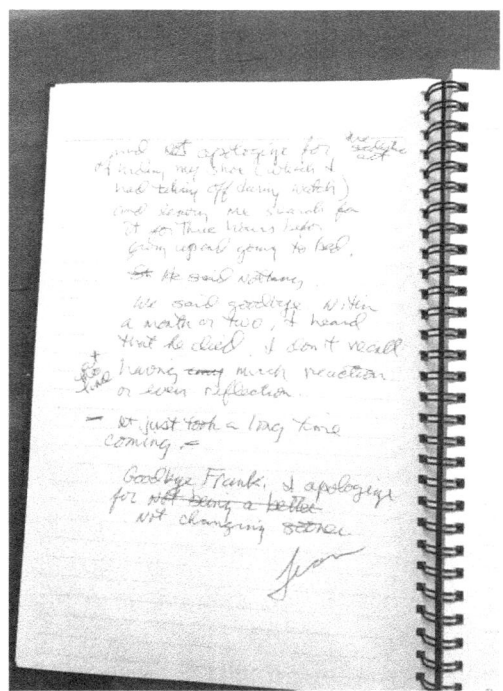

...and *not* apologize for the sadistic act of hiding my shoe (which I had taken off during watch) and leaving me searching for it for three hours before giving up and going to bed.

He said nothing. We said goodbye.

Within a month or two, I heard he died.

I don't recall, at the time, having much reaction or even reflection.

—It just took a long time coming.—

Goodbye Frank. I apologize for not being a better for not changing sooner.

Liam

The End

About the Author

Bill is originally from upstate New York (Auburn) where he graduated from high school in 1962. He served in the United States Navy in the submarine service as a nuclear electrical technician from 1963 to 1969 after which he continued in Reserve status. He received an honorable discharge as a Lieutenant in 1978.

He earned an undergraduate degree, with honors, from the University of Washington in 1972. For the next twelve years, he taught elementary school, served as president of an education association, and, during this time, obtained an MBA degree.

In 1984, he enrolled as a full-time student at Life Chiropractic College West in the San Francisco Bay area. In 1987, he graduated with honors earning a Doctorate of Chiropractic. He is currently in his thirty-first year of practice in Little Rock, Arkansas.

He is married to Connie, and they have a daughter, Tayren.

Bill physically moved on from the navy, but he has always carried the *Underneath It All* navy submarine experience as part of the foundation of his adult self.

* * *

Thank you for reading my book. If you enjoyed it, won't you please take a moment to leave me a review at your favorite retailer?

Thanks!
William Carbary

Connect with me:

Friend me on Facebook:
https://www.facebook.com/william.carbary.7

Coming soon by Bill Carbary: *Think Like Gods*